The Nettle Spinner

Also by Kathryn Kuitenbrouwer

Way Up

KATHRYN KUITENBROUWER

the Nettle
Spinner

GOOSE LANE

Edited by Laurel Boone.
Cover photograph: *Katelyn, Invermere, BC* (detail), 1992, from the series
Shaping the New Forest, by Lorraine Gilbert. Reproduced with permission.
Cover and interior design by Julie Scriver.
Printed in Canada by AGMV Marquis.
This book is printed on acid-free paper that is 100% recycled,
ancient-forest friendly (100% post-consumer recycled).
10 9 8 7 6 5 4 3 2 1

Library and Archives Canada Cataloguing in Publication

Kuitenbrouwer, Kathryn, 1965-
The nettle spinner / Kathryn Kuitenbrouwer.

ISBN 0-86492-422-4

I.Title.

PS8571.U4N48 2005   C813'.6   C2005-900555-6

Published with the financial support of the Canada Council for the Arts, the
Government of Canada through the Book Publishing Industry Development
Program, and the New Brunswick Culture and Sports Secretariat.

Goose Lane Editions
469 King Street
Fredericton, New Brunswick
CANADA E3B 1E5
www.gooselane.com

To
Marc and Linden
Jonas and Christopher

the Nettle spinner

Prologue

≈ The winding sheet that Burchard's wife wrapped around his corpse was slightly off white. It was impossible to tell from a distance what sort of cloth it was. A count of Burchard's status could easily have had a shroud woven from calico or fine Indian cotton. His wife might have had an exquisite damask prepared in one of the mills around Rheims. But, of course, there was Burchard's reputation for thrift, well, tight-fistedness was how the peasants talked of it, and his shroud was already so famous by the time of his death that everyone for miles around knew it was not fashioned from cambric or hemp. It was not dyed with the shells of sea snails nor with indigo or woad (the woad's cross-like flower so fitting for a funeral). It was not fabricated from merino wool nor, for that matter, the cheaper English wool, carded extra fine and woven expertly. No, it was not. It might have been woven by an old peasant woman, one of Burchard's serfs, famous for her skill at transforming simple flax into elegant linen, but it wasn't that either. And it was certainly not silk, spun from a hundred, hundred cocoons. The fibre of the magic shroud was retted from the least noble of all weeds — the stinging nettle.

We are nowhere, northern Ontario. The baby's arms are fat and reaching up to grab. He's ravenous, digs his sharp nails into my breast while he suckles, seems more animal than human. I pull his hand away and nibble the snags off his fingernails. There are aspects of this I can't stand. The sun emerges each morning, makes its slow arc through the sky and drops, like poetry, orange and lively, over the horizon, only to emerge somewhere else, for some other eyes to ponder. I've narrowed my field of vision to this, haven't I? I've chosen it. Well, in any event, chosen something.

My days are simple. I tend the mediocre garden, I weave, or try to, I feed and clean the boy and myself, and I wait. Sometimes, while the boy sleeps in the cabin, I make my way over to the pit, and I stare into the unnatural blue of its water, azure not found anywhere else on earth but here, and I imagine what the descent must have been like, what baubles of gold and glimmering carbuncles were discovered lodged in the deep earth there. In my mind's eye, I watch the miners coming, marching along the curve of the distant hill, mattocks like shadows on their backs, and from this imaginary perspective, I see them as dwarfs tramping a steady path to work, into the sunless cool of the underground. I am mesmerized by the water-filled chute, its artificial vortex that works a sort of vertigo on my nerves, by the dead blue liquid and by the banality of each day as it comes and goes. I stare down with the look of a failed clairvoyant, seeking sight. I stare until the little boy distracts me with his plaintive squeak, his chirrup, his bleat and his needs. I am an unnatural mother but I go to him, automatically.

Chapter One

It is August, hot. I hitch in from the main road; it's been a long somnolent train ride followed by an eye-bobbling bus ride, so far, so far, and I've caught a ride out of Hearst with a trucker aptly named Rudy who banters on his CB radio about the beaver he has tucked in beside him, i.e. me. I feel myself becoming an object, an iconic Canadian object, sure, worth about five cents. It is good to be an object; it releases me from thought. I am a nickel, and worthy.

It's difficult to navigate up north with all these rough, little-used roads, these temporary arteries to obscure wooded (and de-wooded) bug-infested limbs. And yet I manage. Rudy stops the rig and, with a lurching, lustful grope between my legs, lets me off at last season's treeplanting camp, his maniacal laughter receding only after the dust settles and I am alone. Arrived. I take stock. There is the repeating circular evidence of a dome tent village, yellow and white wormy-looking grass patches in strange random groupings, tiny crop circles of recent anthropology, and over there, further, is Willem's tent site, a skinny rectangle of dead grass, his old pup. Can I smell him? I walk through the field as if the entire cornucopic cult were still here and finally pitch my tent back up in its same old spot and settle for the night. Tomorrow will be a grand walk deep into the past, and I need my rest.

I wake up early, my arm numb from sleeping on it. The dead weight of it is like a bad thought, a misdeed, and it is all I can do to slowly release it from its neural paralysis, shaking it out. The inside of my tent is hot and humid; a pretty amber light is held there as if the tent is a vessel full of it. I eat from a supply of dried fruit I have packed, and as I do so, the true meaning of what I am doing here begins to sink in, as fear will if let. I pack up my things and glance around one last time, hoping for company against the facts as they are so clearly laid out before me. A bird would do, but I hear nothing. There is an occasional rustling as chipmunks and other small rodents make their escape from me. I walk toward the old mine clearing, recalling here an odd-shaped shrub and there a weather-stunted tree, ones I've seen before and which now infuse my journey with nostalgia. And so I experience a blunted, hopeful anxiety not unlike excitement, not unlike dread. It does not seem safe to be alone out here, and I consider that I might be insane or that I could be in an extended fugue state from which I may awake refreshed.

The deeper into the bush I go the less sense my plans make, certainly, and my entire life seems suddenly over-dramatized; at several points on the long walk I almost turn back. I find myself singing to pass the time and keep imagined predators at bay. My backpack is heavy, my arm has woken up but still tingles from time to time, not painful but dully aching. This sensation passes by late afternoon, when the pool comes into view. Willem and I first found the ghost town together. We came across it one evening after a long day's planting, late in the season, the sun high in the early summer sky and the bugs alert, spurred into a frenzy, a breeding hunger, by the cooler dusk air. We stopped the ATV and solemnly anointed one another with citronella. And then we continued over potholes and streams that had broken out of their man-made channels and formed rivulets across the abandoned road. The joyride, the gift of Willem's uncle, Ortwin, was a fast-moving escape from the incessant bug life. Our clothes were caked with mud by the time we found the place. The pool, the tiniest edge of which caught our eyes fifty metres into the old gravel clearing, intrigued us, and we stopped the quad and went to it.

The gravel was so thick nothing grew there. The clearing was like a great dead oasis, a lost civilization in the middle of nowhere. The pool, unfathomably deep, was shaped like a funnel, the tube of which, so deep yet so clearly visible underwater, was an old copper mine shaft. This receded into nightmare blackness, a black inactive endlessness. The water, for the rest, was the blue-green of a penny picked up along the curb, and in it too nothing grew. No plant life, no fishes. It was beautiful with the poised elegance of industrial artifice.

It is a woman, Willem had said.

Only as rendered by a man, I muttered back.

The area around the pool was strangely quiet, without the teeming omnipresence of blackflies. It was the stillest water I had ever encountered, and yet no larvae wriggled at its stagnant edges. We held one another for some time, gathering in the poignancy of whatever message it sought to give us. I recall I pressed myself against Willem's long leg, enjoying that soft on hard. What was it exactly that made us turn around, except we were entranced? The little shack stood just there, and we laughed because it represented our deepest separate wishes made manifest. It offered a framework for what we intended to do in it. You'd think they might have built a better town with all the standing timber up there. But from inside we saw it was all planks, set side-by-side and insulated with more planks placed horizontally. I looked out between the boards at the sun-bleached sky, the swirl of blackflies and the heaps of fallen structures, the splintered, grey-weathered shards of previous lives, and then not, and then again, as my perspective moved with our breath, in and out.

So, this is Canada? he said, post-coital, bare-legged. This great land.

Yeah. True north strong. I sifted through his trousers for tobacco. Oh, the smell of him, that smell that completed me.

It is chaos, the empty space, he said. The bugs. The wasted land. The sky falling all the way down to the ground. Everything moving around so mean, so pretty, so free, and in the middle, this — what we just have together. He gestured, then, at his penis.

Um, Willem? I said. It's in your own mind. We have cities here too.

No. Just this. This is the Canada I want. I will come back here, right here.

He wanted so badly to make the particular the universal, to make nature into a symbol, make the bugs mean something, make his come important. This is my last memory of him — seed, Drum, earth, sweat.

I yelp when I see it again and I run toward it. It does not respond. I am alone. I am alone. Alone. All of a sudden I wonder, Now, why did I want to be alone, again? What colossal pretence suggested itself to me that I would behave so? Am I destined to react with such insufferable sensitivity to every life experience? It is true, I returned home. I packed up my apartment, I gave my landlord notice. I wanted to run away, see what that was like, running away. And now I was alone. Alone in this godless place. Alone. Alone. What did it mean? If one was alone, was one, in fact, there at all? Had I ceased to exist? I decide to yell and check for an echo.

Hello! Hello!

Hello! I turn toward the weird echo, for I am not alone. I scan the forest periphery looking for movement, a flash of colour, anything, and I see him. A little man sits on a stump in front of a shack I'd not noticed before. It is behind the other hut and hidden by the scrub edge of the forest so as to be completely camouflaged. The leprechaun grins at me.

Haven't I seen you before? he says.

I blink to check my senses. He grins wider, and his little eyes completely disappear into leathery crow's feet.

Fuck, I think. Damn. I come all this way, and still. This cannot be real.

Welcome, there. He's holding up his little hand by way of greetings.

Hullo? This is certainly a hallucination.

I am Jake, he says, pointing to himself.

Are you real?

That's right. You bet. And you? He laughs; he is laughing at me.

Huh?

Your name is?

Alma. Listen, who are you? How long have you been here? What's this . . .

I'm not here, he interrupts, holds his miniature hand up again. And then he breaks out into peal upon peal of shrill laughter, his chin pressed into his ragged old quilted corduroy coat. The man is shaking with laughter. I look up and see Willem's underwear waving from a pole attached to his shack.

Sweet Jesus.

They are mottled pink bikinis, inadvertently dyed once when they got into a dark load. Willem. I am back in the little hut with Willem, right here, right here. I'm weak in the legs thinking about him, for these thoughts go to obvious places. Willem had jumped up and gone outside in order to find a stick. He was triumphant, came back waving it at me. Tobacco smoke went down my windpipe when I laughed, and I choked and coughed. Willem tied his pink garment to one end of the stick and hoisted his rigged flag up against the structure.

I claim this place. Right here, he announced. I stare, reminiscing.

Jake, the little man is saying again, Jake. I am Jake. I am not here. I am not sweet Jesus, either.

Oh, I see. I say this though I don't, not really.

You understand, then. Yes. Good. Now, you must come in. You are my first visitor in one hundred years and I'm very lonely. Come in. Come in, please.

Jake gets up and grabs my bicep with both his hands, walks me into the hut, brings me up to every wall and points to his things. It is the cabin of a man with poor eyesight and little concern for hygiene. Filthy. There is a lingering reek of rotting food and badly cured animal skins. These skins are stacked against the wall in anticipation of cold weather. A massive unmortared fireplace takes up the rest of this wall. There are two rooms and three windows. One screened window in the bedroom, south wall, one in the kitchen above the old corroded sink and hand pump, again south wall, one in the main living area, that is to say, the rest of the house, east wall. Each of these has a collection of found anthropology laid out on its sill — animal craniums, feathers, strange rocks, old salve bottles, tins — talismans of what? There is a table, rather ornate considering where it sits, and I wonder how it got here. There is a Findlay Oval cookstove, missing legs and so propped up on little cairns.

The yellow walls are gorgeous. He has parged them with some sort of chinking and painted the place in a thin ochre, which is brighter at the floor, as if the walls are actually draining of colour. I hadn't seen this particular structure before. I'd anticipated making house in the smaller shelter, the forlorn little cabin that looks out, windows like eyes, onto the pit; it might have been where the foreman kept warm and dry in inclement weather. The one in which Willem and I made love once, up against the back wall of it, the spruce planks absorbing our thrust. But I know no comfort will be found in that hut. It is bereft of comfort. And everything as I had imagined it suddenly shifts to make room for this yellow shack and for Jake.

I look at him and he becomes self-conscious, begins to move things about in the little kitchen, tidying up like a nervous hostess. I wonder. Jake may have been watching us those months ago, or listening, and had we seen him or heard him we might have thought he was a ghost. Perhaps he thought we were. Perhaps we were — as if the imagined is a sort of ghost, distinct from reality but somehow more tangible. Did I imagine it? And this, this ghost town? I consider, for the last and most profound time, turning back. Simultaneously, I consider my mother brooding in her cups and the tragic dullness of my other life; it unreels before me in convincing panels, negatives. He reads my mind.

You have come to live with me. I will sleep here. He indicates the heap of skins. I take very little room. I am often not around at all. Please. You will have privacy over there. He beckons me to come over to the bedroom. My legs will not move. I will not follow this little man, whoever he is — *if* he is.

I am waiting for someone, I say. I don't even believe this anymore, not really. I will talk myself around again, even in the face of a bastion of pragmatics. I will reconstruct faith as it suits me.

No one comes here, he says.

I know.

But I know this too. Something will happen here. There is an event in motion. It swirls around this locus, right here. I must, I will stay and see it through.

Chapter Two

❧ It was autumn. The fields were golden stubble,
the stooked flax would soon be brought to the river-
side and soaked until the outer wood softened and
stank and disintegrated so that the retters could get
to work and draw out the woolly linen. The burial
entourage made a parade through the fields. The
maidens were dressed in white, like virgin brides,
witnesses to the dead's now presumed innocence.
The bishop was there, mitred, dressed in the shiny
vestments — flashing red, blood-red — that he
wore each spring during the benediction of the
fields. He had administered extreme unction the
day before, as Burchard finally collapsed onto the
just-finished shroud, kissing the little hand of the
girl-weaver Renelde in gratitude. Strange to think
a twelve-year-old girl could weave so finely; strange,
too, to see sweet youth standing in the midst of
putrid death.

Since the cloth was wound around the corpse,
it was impossible to see the thing of a piece.
Only Renelde, her grandmother and her great-
grandmother, who all lived together in a little
fieldstone cottage on the edge of the forest, had
witnessed the progress of the death garb. Renelde's
mother was long dead of a strange illness no one,
not even the ancient healer, had been able to cure.

So just these three and one more knew what story wove its way through the threads of that shroud.

Burchard's wife, she had seen it too. These four had the luxury of time before the thing was laid out and wrapped about the anointed cadaver. These four had marvelled at the intricacy of the weaving, the subtle details — white on white, shuttled in with ever-so-finely spun nettle thread — of his life and Renelde's and how these twined around one another.

Even the strange becomes normal over time. I move in, occupy the bedroom, and out of wariness behave queenly and austere. Jake laughs whenever clumsiness or inexperience blows my cover. I don't trust him because I don't know him, and I can't know him because I don't trust him. He is ancient, so old he's lost his gender and looks like an old woman, an apple doll, a shrunken head. He disappears for days and returns with groceries, for which I am running out of money (he steals from me while I steel myself against him). I'll have to make a decision soon, I know. Time is passing.

Shit or get off the pot. Jake yells this to me every morning when I go seeking privacy.

Waiting is fraught with neurotic inclination, weakness of personality, amplified tragic flaws, bereavement, longing, inertia and pure love. I've begun weaving the story cloth, reciting and recreating the old story in fragments. This focuses my work. Maybe there is something magical in the battening down of thread on a loom. The nettle thread is as silk, strong and delicate. It lies in tautly wrapped clews at my feet. I draw it through the warp, and thud-thud, thud-thud, the rhythm draws me in. Evelyn taught me well; the threads are true and the images emerge livelier than they would on a page. My Nettle Spinner cloth will recount the story in its totality, panel by panel, like an oblique cartoon. This first panel is bordered with a pattern, a cheeky reconstructed nettle leaf repeater. The central image is the corpse wrapped tightly. The nettle thread I have used here is very fine and elsewhere rougher, so that the body seems to float on a square of gossamer. It is astonishing. The beauty of it chills my heart. Jake peers over my shoulder, gasps and puts his tiny hand over his mouth.

What is it? he says.

It's an old story.

Tell me.

I tell him a little bit and then I stop. I don't want him to have any more. He urges me to go on, starts poking my shoulder, but I shake my head and tell him I have to keep working and to leave me alone.

Later. Later, I say.

He snarls vaguely at me. There are many varieties of escape, he says.

We have had some time by now to get to know one another, and I am not taken in by his snarl. Jake likes buoyancy and all things lighthearted. His mood is put on, a manipulation. I attend my weaving, leaning back to create tension. The loom I have is simple and attaches by a strap around my back; I hook the other end to a bent nail I've hammered into the wall. When all the panels are complete, I will sew them together into an episodic quilt. It will be an abstraction of infinity, a repeating image. It will be the shroud telling the story of the shroud, which tells the story of the shroud. Conceptually, it will be like the picture on the cocoa tin that is perched on the kitchen shelf. The tin shows a sexy nun holding a tin of Droste Dutch chocolate, detailing a smaller sexy nun holding a tin of Droste, and so on.

I do miss good cocoa. The tin is empty. I chew on chicory root when I can find it. Jake is crouching in the corner by the door; now I've put him off. He's come back recently from a grocery run, two days missing. He pulls out a Kit-Kat, unwraps it and waves it about. The smell of it entices me so I let the weaving drop onto the mattress and go to him. We are vultures when it comes to chocolate. Later, we'll suffer through generic hot chocolate, which is overly sweet and underly chocolate. Jake and I agree on this. He is old enough to have tasted hot cocoa on the *Titanic*, or so he claims. Stowaway — he claims that too. And I can almost picture him there, huddled in the engine room, his face camouflaged by a smear of machine oil, his hand snatching at dropped morsels and, late in the night, his body surreptitiously locating the scullery, enjoying a respite from hiding, two chilled palms cupping a mug of purloined choco; the ecstasy of a yearning fulfilled plays across his face.

In essence, Jake is a stowaway. It is his theme, if a person can be said to have one. He is furtive and sneaky, as if the very act of stowing himself on the ill-fated ship was itself predestined. He is a thief of small inconsequential spaces, of physical gaps, and what he steals is barely noticed, like what a mouse steals, yet the effect is felt in ripples and causes untold fear, for what is a stowaway to the captain of an epic boat but fear of the unknown? Fear embodied. Also, Jake's got one foot in the grave and what's more he always has had. He hides between a rock and a hard place, neither here nor there, relying on everyone's forgiving nature. He hid on the ship, then on the lifeboat.

Jake has a sugar rush, a fit of the giggles, and then he crashes. Oh, he is old and horrid. Better, he is old, therefore horrid. I will nurture this revulsion. Jake is dangerous. He loves to disappear. I'm scared of him, but one must make use of fear. I watch him sleep on his heap of skins, and I find myself shuddering in anticipation of his usefulness. I look out the kitchen window. I see the smaller structure. I see the edge of the sunken mine shaft pool, the vestiges of this dead town, wooden monuments, collapsed structures. And beyond, the anorexic forest one finds this far north, what dares to grow on permafrost and shield or what is forced upon this earth — only tenacious trees. And beyond that, the sky, its clouds drifting elsewhere, away.

The cold is upon us before the last summer sun drops. September brings snow, and as I look desperately out the door, the wind hurling it over the threshold, Jake cackles.

All the convenience of a deep-freeze, he says. City folk pay for that.

We have made a trail over to behind the hut, making our regular trips there so that the snow stays packed. I am heaping mittfuls of snow to hide my creation. A sudden thought: God created Adam out of mud, did he not? What is mud but the most primal of creations? Shit and life itself. Shit or get off the pot, indeed. There is little separating life and death, creation and destruction. In between, there is only routine. Through the early winter, I weave in the morning while the early day gives me light. I weave and feed the hearth. For reasons of light and warmth, I've moved my work into the main room. There is a small stack of cloth forming beside me. Jake comes and goes, bringing food and forcing me into conversation, into his past, as if speaking of it is retributive.

My arm was broken, he says, trying to draw me in.

I roll my eyes. We've been through this territory ad nauseam. How he wrapped himself in a shawl and pulled a party dress out of that red leather valise, the one that didn't belong to him, just as nothing belonged to him anymore, and he tugged it on, in horror, absolute horror that he had to stowaway again. The ship offered no salvation, no escape, only waves and waves of brutal, piercingly cold water. He disappeared into that act and only emerged an hour out, made a sad go of it with the oar but had to relinquish everything. For the pain. The pain! They did not count him as a passenger. He wasn't a paid fare. He was historically insignificant, not entered onto any list. The arm broke with the lurch of the ship itself as it filled with ice-cold water and heaved in two.

Like the ship, he says, I broke.

He wags his head while he speaks to me. His eyes are trying to find my crisp outline. He does not see well.

I'm not your crutch, I say. I'm not interested in helping him come to terms with this crime.

It was a broken arm, he says, not a broken leg!

My pregnancy is announced mid-January. I recall the wind beating against the shack, the thin walls barely able to withstand it, the construction shuddering and seeming to wave about as if we were on the open sea. Jake notices first. It comes as a shock to admit my belly has expanded, to come to terms with the eventuality of a labour, a child. I didn't ask for this. There were signs I ignored for too long, the missed periods I believed due to starvation, the strange foreign thrum of life I mistook for diarrhea. The equation for pregnancy is not so random, I know, and I ought to have considered this possibility, but, as bent as I was on re-establishing myself in this phantomscape, this wretched undone land, it did not enter my mind until, having made something of a friendship, however tempestuous, with Jake, and fattened up on whatever kill he brought home, and he is pretty adept at the hunt, I could no longer avoid the obvious changes my body was undergoing. I'm not keen on motherhood; it has been thrust upon me. Jake tries to convince me that I ought to leave, but leaving is not really an option. The snow is past my hips in some places and escape will certainly seal my fate. I figure I have until March, that I'll get out then.

I foretell a son, he says. Jake has grabbed my hand and dangled a threaded needle over my open palm.

Wha?

Really, three boys over time. Three sons and one daughter, later. I stare at him.

It's a lie, he admits. There will be no daughter. I only wanted to see you smile.

I do not smile. I piece together the facts while watching the needle make diminishing circlets in space below his garden-callused paw, wondering exactly what this might mean, and how I might fit into that same meaning. I wish I could say I find myself falling instantly in love with this self within myself. I do not. I am spooked, even more so in realizing that there is nowhere to run. I look for my wild edibles book and frantically research abortifacients, only to discover I've brought the wrong book. I weave and, dissatisfied, undo my weaving — like Penelope, though without the suitors. She had to keep the horny throng at bay; I must only preserve my limited supply of nettle. I enter the work and successfully ignore my body. I ignore it.

The dead guy, Jake says, what happened to him? He's holding up the corpse panel. His eyes are truly going. I notice him clutching a pair of drugstore reading glasses, which I believe he has stolen on one of his long trips away. They have fantastic black frames, offset with yellowing plastic around the curl where the arms sit on his ears. He puts them on and squints through them at the weaving. His eyes are inches from the cloth. He acts as if he doesn't resent it that I've more or less taken over the cabin. He acts as if he wanted this. There are a hundred, hundred ways in which he has shown he doesn't like my presence, yet we are bound, tethered by the communal fear we share of the wilderness and its encroachment.

> ✳ A little boy stood tugging at the edge of the
> shroud. What's it say? What's it say? Renelde
> had to unclasp his little fingers from the cloth
> and pull him away. Do you know the story? he
> begged. What happened to Burchard the Wolf?

Chapter Three

✳ The Forêt de Mormal was a vast expanse of greenery; trees sprouted easily and grew like weeds. There were hedge beeches, the bark growing so rapidly year by year that it broke open into a series of rough parallelograms to allow for new growth, moss green framed with an almost skin-like pink. The beeches were monolithic, immense, their roots heaving out of the ground to drink the very air, itself almost as humid as the earth in which the roots sought stability. Shelves of shaggy-hair moss and glossy ivy edged up the north side of each tree, even the little new-growth trees. Parasitic mistletoe formed ethereal spheres, strange nest-like structures in the upper branches, as many as five or six in a tree; these grew up the oaks, the poplars. And little streams cut through the forest in meanders, switching back erratically over the years, as if they too were alive, pulling saplings into their intention, creating roadways and bridges over which small animals crossed.

The peasants were free to glean tisanes and medicinals, but the wild boar, the pheasant and grouse, the deer were the property of Burchard and off-limits to anyone but him. Hunting was Burchard's only activity; otherwise he lounged in boredom, listening to his advisers reel off the taxes levied on imported wool bales, the productivity lists regarding flax and hemp cultivation — in short, the dull banality of wealth easily accrued. That day at the edge of the forest, his dead roe bleeding on the ground at the hooves of the palfrey, when he first saw the white, unblemished cheek of Renelde, Burchard was given something he never expected to have outside the fantasy of old women's fairy tales — a quest.

He settled his horse and yelled at her, What is your name, girl-child? She did the worst thing she could have done under the circumstances; just as the deer had before her, she turned and ran away. Oh, Burchard was skilled in the art of venery! He relished the chase. Renelde was a flash of brown cloth, an unformed child, there was a line of freckles along the bridge of her nose, her hair was brown going to black. Burchard laughed at her apprehension and the anxiety, the animal fear she displayed in fleeing. He reined his wife's horse in (his own had ringworm, had been sequestered in the stables and salved with a walnut compress). At a slow trot he pursued the little girl, followed her home and was satisfied only when she turned and stared at him, up so high upon that damp horse. She slipped over the threshold of the cottage and shut the door. He dismounted, grinning.

It was the old woman who answered his rap. She was stooped from sitting at the loom so many years. Her skin was pale from lack of light, like a leek mounded up in the soil, white like a leek. A vague acrid smell wafted off her, the smell of noxious dye; her hands were criss-crossed with wrinkles,

etched and accentuated with madder, cochineal
when it could be obtained, and nettle green.

Who is the girl? Burchard demanded.

The old woman's hand was clutching the
door. She had dandled Renelde in her arms only
yesterday, so it seemed. She was not rancorous.
It was not to be considered an affront when the
count of the land came calling on a peasant girl.
It wasn't that she didn't like or approve of Guilbert
the woodcutter, Renelde's betrothed — he was a
fine and honest individual — but if the child was
of interest to a man of means, then so be it. Burchard puffed out his chest to make himself more
substantial.

Has she misbehaved? the old woman asked.

Send her out; I want to be alone with her.

Jake brags occasionally about his prowess as an obstetrician.
Doctor, he says, tapping his chest and winking. It is a lie. He was
howling like a coyote outside the door, in rhythm with my
tortured, moaning contractions. Okay, I'll give him that last, he
did make a lot of noise. Though I can't see how it could have
helped. I was more or less alone. It's not the sort of thing one
should do alone, give birth, but the boy came early and I was
unprepared. I had a sense that my self had abandoned me, and
this feeling did not give way when the boy arrived. For all he is
beautiful and pleasant, these details only exacerbate my fury. And
to add insult to injury, I also love him, cannot help but love him,
in some chemical bond that nothing seems to sever. Through the
spring, I try leaving him behind at the pit, but his little momen-
tous trills bring me running back. I am his hostage just as he is mine.

He hasn't any teeth yet and is too young for mashed burdock,
but he's hungry. He sucks at me with the ferocity of someone

uncertain of his worth, with a furrowed brow, with a presentiment of my distaste. Jake walks by chuckling, as usual, a dead rabbit, skinned and gutted, hanging by a leather rope down by his side, flopsy ears skimming the ground. He's eyeing my tit and stops to poke the boy with his bloodied finger. The child breaks suction. Jake does it on purpose so he can expose my nipple and get a good look. The baby pushes a bit of blue-white milk out his mouth as he approximates a laugh. Jake's mouth opens empathetically and pulses a bit as if in a dream; missing teeth, he is the baby suckling. I cover myself quickly.

Go fuck yourself.

Too old, he says, and rubs the boy's belly. Milk is shooting out of my nipple and wetting my clothing.

Go get the Findlay going then. Get dinner. Would you?

He does. I can hear the crackle of dry kindling behind me, and it isn't long before my back is warm from the radiant heat. The rabbit will be a feast. The boy latches on again and drinks me in. I expect his eyes to close but they don't. I swaddle him and lay him down under the table so Jake won't accidentally step on him, and I set to weave until the meat can be eaten. I look up from time to time and see Jake peering at me, swaying back and forth. He looks like a fucking idiot. I start to think about Karl, rocking in the back of the orange treeplanting crummy-van, the stink mobile. I must work, I must work to form *this*, so *that* will not take hold.

The panel I'm working on has a staggered forest in the background; a girl-weaver, Renelde, stares straight out, in the act of drawing fibre from a bundled distaff down into thread, onto a twirling spindle. I have tried my best to render her without expression but, in fact, she looks like me, skewed hair tamed by braids, skeptical about the eyes. Jake is right, my weaving is a distraction. History repeats itself. I take solace that Jake has not figured out that the weaving is also a compulsion and, like all compulsions, dangerous in its consequences. As I work, I feel myself recede. I am a blur, a swathe of dull, dirty brown, from which a voice projects. I catch a whiff and stop work. There is an unmistakable odour floating through the hut.

What's that smell, Jake? I say.

Dinner.

No. It smells like shit. Is that ours?

No, wolf, maybe?

They're hungry, no doubt; they smell the rabbit cooking. I'm looking out the window, scanning the perimeter of the forest; nothing.

It's the boy they're after — little, unprotected.

Jake's at me about my maternal instinct or lack thereof. Fuck him. I count off my fingers at him. Near-blind, I say. Stupid. Inconsequential. Don't worry, you'll be the first to go.

He shakes his head at me, the tiniest hint of a laugh on his upper lip. You ought to carry the bastard, he says. He spits this, really. You ought never to leave him alone. It's sick the way you do that. A real mother doesn't do like that. You carry him. You should . . .

I stop listening. But I know Jake loves the boy like a father. Like he thinks a father might love a son. When he's around. Jake is yelling and tossing plates and food onto the table. It's upsetting. The baby lets out a deep roar of disapproval, pulls its feet into its stomach again and again, and then he craps himself. It resounds as an insult. It resounds as a thwack of thick liquid against a wall.

You see, I say. You woke him up.

Ah, the little bastard. Jake starts to giggle.

He holds onto his own crotch; Jake pees himself regularly when he laughs. The whole hut by winter's end smells of dried urine. I lean over and grab a square of sheeting, what I use for diapers, and throw it at him, catching him across the face. The cloth shows him in relief as a gauzy stain-streaked ghost. His laughing gasp sucks the material into the cave of his mouth and he closes his teeth around it, still grinning. I see he's grabbed the boy's ankle and drawn him closer. He's waving a safety pin in the air already. The boy's wide eyes swirl around trying to follow the motion.

Hurry, the meat will be cold.

I watch him slip off the boy's swaddling and peer into the diaper, making a face. The shuttle goes back and forth, the threads tighten. Jake's hand wipes the cherubic ass, legs kicking, the earnest expression on Jake's face, the shuttle opening and closing. I can see the scene on the cloth forming, its rude snubbing, its amateurish representation still pleasing.

Don't call him a bastard, I say.

Why not? It's true, he is.

It feels like bad luck, is all.

I have an idea, Jake says, leaning over and rubbing my cheek facetiously with the back of his hand.

Oh?

My idea is this. I'm the father.

I'm laughing only I'm not, I say.

Well, I might as well be. What did he look like?

Who?

You know. The real father.

I want to say, He looked like a dwarf of Hapsburg lineage, the dwarfism manifested through some misrepresentation of a bad-gene-carrying third cousin. A tragedy. I want to say he was a spinner by trade, one who desperately, desperately wanted to pass on the family name. Grimm. But I know he won't get the reference to Rumpelstiltskin and I'm not in the right mood. I almost tell him about Willem but I feel hurt by that too. It demonstrates my impracticality. The level of failure I've attained. Even in failure I am ambitious.

It was dark, I say. I didn't get a good look.

Chapter Four

Jake asks me to tell him about treeplanting. I tell him about the first time. It is a safe story. I was twenty, visiting a friend one morning, when his overnight guest came down the stairs, saying, Hello, goodbye. He stood there momentarily in the diffused light of early May. The gleam softened the military appearance of his khaki army pants, the olive drab, many-pocketed surplus jacket. From his massive backpack hung a dibble shovel, but I didn't know the name for it yet. Planting sacks, along with other necessities of wilderness living, were strapped on with a criss-cross of colourful bungee cords. I wanted him. No. I wanted to be him. Whatever it was *he* was, I wanted that.

What are you? I said.

Where am I going, you mean?

No, what are you? A soldier?

No. I'm a treeplanter. He shifted his pack and his chest puffed out.

A what?

Johnny Appleseed, he said. Only with trees.

I scoured the want ads, and when I saw, some days later, a small, semi-literate advertisement for treeplanters, no exp. nec., will train, I called and enthusiastically declared my adeptness at gardening, thrilling to my own air-brushed rendering of a weekend I'd spent years before hauling gravel and stone screenings around the family home with my mother and father and laying an appalling interlock patio. I proclaimed myself to be a hard worker, and the man at the other end seemed to believe me.

I found out later that the only reason he hired me was to keep Esther, his underfed girlfriend, company. Together, over a platter of fries and ketchup at a little diner called Mars, he and Esther interviewed me. Could they not hear from the shrill falseness in my eager voice that I had no idea?

Here's a list of things, they said.

Things?

Yes, you'll need them.

With three college boys and a collie-shepherd-spaniel dog and all the gear, I piled into the back of a double-cab panel truck which, it turned out, was borrowed from an uncle for the season, with admonishments that it not be scratched. We drove and drove, deep into Canada. I acted natural, while Esther, in the front passenger seat, turned around to tell us of her various allergic sensitivities, including milk, eggs and nuts, sunshine, dust, wheat and possibly corn, and that there better be a health food store where we were going. Otherwise, she didn't know what she was going to do.

Oh and bee sting, she said. But I keep a kit, so don't you worry.

We drove and drove. Day gave way to night, the sky was blue then black. The forest was a jagged blackness against the black. We followed the road's sway, the inertial pull of curving highway pressing us into one another. I fell in and out of droning sleep and half-caught conversation, excited and exhausted in the getting-to-know-you-all phase of the thing, gauging my ability to live in close quarters with these people. By journey's end, I hated Esther and also one of the college boys, who played a great deal of tennis and studied Russian and filled the truck cab with a brooding Bolshevik atmosphere. He may have been mad.

We are going to Siberia, you know? he kept saying. It will be cold; it will be deathly miserable. Do you know what they think of women in Siberia? He stared at me with a darkened look, which I mistook for humour. I burst out laughing.

They kill the women like *that* when they discover them. First they rape, he said, moving his hands up and down some imaginary body. Then they kill, he continued. You're a fool to come here.

The fourteen-hour drive had given me a jarring, hallucinatory inner hum. I hummed. Early morning mist rose in wisps from the earth. The truck pulled into a small clearing, into the landscape of deforestation. We were on a logging road an hour's drive deep in the backwoods, the dust just settling. A Ministry of Natural Resources truck was waiting for us. The forester got out and pointed into the bush with his shovel. He handed us each a treebag, a slung-over-the-shoulder affair, not unlike an old postal sack, along with a heavy utility shovel. It was the antithesis of the gear I witnessed on my iconic treeplanter, that stranger at my friend's house, the vision I had maintained of tree-planterness.

I geared up as best I could and began to walk. I walked as if in a dream that was all too real. The mud stuck to my boots and pulled me down into the earth. We walked for an hour through quagmires, bramble and nettle over ungraded pathways deeper and deeper into the bush; we followed the squelch of tire tracks, the stink of upturned earth for kilometres, forest on either side, the birds within crying out their worry and dismay. They had seen figures like us before. I tried to keep up with the others, to remain cool, to relax into the desperation I felt.

Then the forest began to dwindle in the most horrific manner. Spruce and pine had been plowed over in heaps along the edge of the woods. Corridors became suddenly apparent, formed by the massacre of other trees now pushed aside in rows. I looked hard into these strange alleyways, trying to make sense of the destruction. Stumps had been brutally ripped from the earth and turned upside down into piles, no trees standing. The land rose and fell in sublime hills and valleys, its skin tortured, scarified, scarred by ridges of debris which had been cleared away to facilitate our work. A large bull moose abruptly turned and ran into the darkness of the far distant forest. The Russian student whispered under his breath.

We will overtake them by sundown, he said. Esther giggled nervously.

It was the silence that amazed me, the expansive quietness of it. The birds seemed to have evacuated this place. It was empty. I weighed the cost of my gear against turning back. Which way to go? I looked around and knew I could not leave. I was trapped, in debt for hundreds of dollars from the purchases I had made. A sensation of agoraphobia overcame me. I had never been so exposed before, so in the open, so impossibly imprisoned by the wide world. The Russian student stood slightly behind Esther and the crew boss. He was crying. The others milled about like a herd, kicking at clumps of earth, pressing their shovels into the frozen ground. I imagined a frisson to our collective fear and felt a sudden, unaccountable kinship with these people. We turned, as eager flowers to the sun, and stared at the man who had hired us. He wore a baseball cap that I suddenly recognized as silly, infantile, worrisome and worn backwards. What appealed to me about this man? Why had I trusted him? How did I know he had brought me here for the express purpose of planting trees? What sick plot might be in store for me? And then, why did I want this exactly? Why was I so persuasively intrigued by that stranger in a doorway, that sun-drenched unknown with his military demeanour and his claim to the legacy of some eccentric American orchardist?

We were taught the T cut and then the L cut, all with our ludicrous government-issue shovels, weighing a ton. I desperately tried to make these cuts swiftly while simultaneously finding room in the little hole I had made for the endless, overgrown sapling taproot. I wound the devilish appendage carefully around itself and tried to keep the ground open long enough to set it gently in, my coordination tried to the limits of Atlas, holding up not the sky but the earth, even this little speck of it, trying beyond its *own* willingness to nurture.

Why should I penetrate this body? Who asked me to interfere? And for all that, I persevered. Inside a week, I went from earning a dollar seventy-five a day to earning twenty-one dollars. I enjoyed an idealism that was unconvincing in light of the trouble to which I was being put. I knew nothing, understood nothing of what I was doing. I did not know, for instance, that these tree saplings were harvested from one mother tree, that they were über-trees. If one happened to carry disease, they would all die. I believed myself to be nature's little helper. My naïveté was astounding. It slowed me down. I stopped and smiled at the pretty trail of trees and a feeling of quaint smugness washed over me. It was only halfway through the season, when I put that idealism away, that do-goodery, that saving Mother Earth, that I began to earn above my camp costs.

He left the contract early. The Russian student. He came out of the woods one day wearing a pith helmet covered in a faded, Muskol-doused red T-shirt. He held his shovel as if it was a rifle and fell to the ground like a young boy, making the sound of machine-gun fire somewhere in the space at the back of his throat, reeling back in fake agony as the enemy bullets hit him about the shoulders. He screamed in realistic mortal pain. And his tent and his gear were gone next day, and no one mentioned him much after that. He merely disappeared, leaving the good fight to us. It was just Esther and the others then, Esther and her lack of health food, her slowly thinning physique, her declared missed periods, her nervous high-pitched laugh, her standing around proffering macerated reconstituted ham out of a roll-top tin.

Eat, she said. Eat. No allergens!

There were two types of treeplanters. The ones who came for one season and never returned and the others, who were seduced by something in the air, some drive to be bushwhacked, something primal. I was the latter. In time, I learned to think only of myself. I learned to replace the righteousness of planet nurturing with a bleak Darwinism. I began to form a hierarchy in which I was at the top. I persevered. Esther, on the other hand, had more or less given up earning anything. She contented herself by doing odd jobs for her crew-boss lover, cutting slices of ham and preparing sandwiches for the rest of us. I stared rudely, defiantly at that Spam outstretched toward me in friendly supplication. It was human weakness, sloth, self-indulgence and small-mindedness. Eager for a tidbit, the yappy dog ran around and around Esther's legs.

Chapter Five

No girl had ever been so ingloriously wooed. Burchard hoisted her onto the horse and mounted behind her, pushed his spurs into the poor animal's flank and set off at a pace that reminded Renelde of the hurtling she sometimes experienced just as sleep overcame her. The horse sidled through the forest trees, unperturbed by the bramble that tore at its legs. Burchard stopped short somewhere in the very depths of the forest, in a place that Renelde had never ventured, off the various paths on which the peasants and the gentry travelled to and fro. He pulled her off the horse and told her she was exquisite, a word with which she was not familiar. He gently brushed the hair off her cheek. Her face was flushed with fear. He then did what any man will do if he has never learned self-restraint.

His breath calmed when his lust was satisfied and had given way to light caresses down her unformed breast. You must come and live with me in the castle, as my wife's maid, he said.

She shook her head. I cannot, sir. I love the countess too much for that, and besides I am betrothed. Renelde lay as still as if she were dead.

Ah, but my wife has a welcoming soul, Burchard said. And as for your betrothal, that is easily unravelled. I insist you come; I can no more

live without you than . . . well, now I know you.
He leaned into her and kissed her breast as if it
was a meal laid upon his very own table. She had
no new answer for him. Her only answer was already
offered. That he had taken what was not his to
take did not enter his mind. The land and all that
grew upon it was his. It infuriated him that she did
not bend to his birthright. Her implacability enraged
him. He followed her for days and cornered her in
unlikely places and begged her, once with genuine
tears flowing down his face. She was the most pure,
modest, beautiful creature he had ever laid his eyes
on. She was unattainable. Burchard forced his hand
with her, in the name of love, a sentiment that
overran him, caused him profound grief the likes
of which he had never before imagined. It cut him,
wounded him, afflicted him, drained him of all his
energy and, simultaneously, energized him. No one
had ever said no to him before.

Come and live in my castle, he insisted. I will
make you maid-in-waiting to the countess.

She shook her head.

Once upon a time. The story I don't tell Jake. The story that isn't
safe to tell: the shovel went in, the earthen hole gaped, the tree
root was buried. A careless operation. It seemed like ages ago,
but it had been only one year since I last joined the ranks of the
wayward, the hippies, the avaricious, ambitious university
brigade and the cultish Bhagwan Rajneesh groupies, their orange
clothing so lively in the early morning frost of Hearst, Ontario,
in May and June. I would do again what I had first done four
summers before, and each summer since — plant spindly little
conifers just south of the treeline, each tree a back-crunching
effort, earning seven to ten cents per, not to mention athlete's

foot, callused hips and thighs, a certain infection due to blackfly bites, DEET burns along the neck and shoulders, an oozing staphylococcus someone had brought back from Egypt, various bruises, scratches down the legs and arms, chafing.

There were really only two rational reasons to treeplant and neither had to do with ecology. The first was purely fiscal. The other was an enduring joy to the job, the joy, once I had become adept at it, of facility, of physical ease. The lyricism of motion. I liked to stop in open burns and watch the other planters stoop and plant and rise, shovels poised, then dropped like spear shafts to the kill. I enjoyed the infinite repetition — the draw, the tree whipped out of the bag, the stoop, the rise, all the while the figure, treeplanter (sun-baked skin, sun-bleached cotton plaid farmer's shirt billowing in the wind), moving silently, erratically away. The ash rose up into little cumulus-like puffs each time the shovel cut the earth. Treeplanting had a compelling physicality I could not replace in other ways, a physicality that made it difficult for me to deny the call each spring — the thick smell of mud, the sexiness of earth drawing me toward it.

I worked for a West Coast firm owned by two Dutch hippies who had tired of the Vancouver pot culture and decided to go entrepreneurial. They saw a niche market in the scarred clearcuts, saw opportunity there in the detritus of forest fire. A year ago, I was glazed over with wanting to go back. I was an addict of soil and hard weather and the erotic momentum of clouds. There were preparations to make, work to be done. Before leaving, I had to clean out the fridge, a shuddering 1975 harvest gold monstrosity full of unmarked leftovers decayed almost to toxicity. I cleaned it out annually as a ritual before I headed up north. This fridge was the focal point of my claustrophobic apartment on the main floor of a chopped-up Edwardian house, a hodge-podge of ad hoc renovations strewn with personal treasures: a great number of paisley scarves, treatises on the history and practice of weaving, old notes from Evelyn's course. The living room sufficed as a bedroom. The bathroom — shower, mini-tub, vanity and all — was constructed, crammed in actually, along the hallway by the stairs to the second floor apartment.

The walls were papered with an ancient woodchip-textured material, painted every six years, whether it needed it or not, in a shiny bluish-white oil-based smear. The kitchen opened onto the dining room, the division marked by an ugly strip of aluminum where linoleum met hardwood. The furniture, table, every surface held books and magazines and tea-stained ceramic mugs, left in situ until they were all dirty and I had to fill the sink and wash them. I was bound to the place by my laziness. By inertia.

Rot. On the top shelf of the fridge, I spotted yogurt fungus, its lacy green foam seeping under the lid and travelling down the outside of the tub. There was a naval orange sinking into a brown puddle in a half-tied plastic sack. A lumpy white circular mould on top of the jam, its peak of forest green forming up the inside wall of the jar. And the smell. The reek was heartbreaking. I had to deal with an entire bowl of desiccated lemons. They had shrivelled and darkened and thinned. The skins were hardened shells not unlike shellacked Easter eggs, and I peeled one. A nugget of pulpy juice, two drops, no more, and one miserable little seed. I felt like crying. My mother called just as I was sorting compost from trash. I ran water into an almost full pint of whipping cream. Stinking lumps gurgled up over the top, pulsing into the stream of chlorinated water. They wobbled in the drain before dispersing.

Alma? she said. Alma, where are you?

Mum? You called me. Where are *you*? I had the cordless phone tucked up between my ear and shoulder and was poking a stiff deposit of fungus with the back end of a wooden spoon in order to facilitate its journey down the drain to Lake Ontario.

Her voice warbled. Home, she said. Home was on the eighteenth floor of a condo building, the Ivory Tower. She moved

there when they divorced, purchasing with her share of the spoils
— yes, it was a war — a quantity of useless and extravagant
furnishings. I imagined her slumped into the feather couch; she
paid a fortune for it, claiming it was the couch my father would
never have permitted her to buy when they were together and
that was why she had to have it. Upholstered in burgundy velvet,
it was the blue-red of royal blood, chosen for its pretence, its
appearance of upper classness, its hopeful snobbery. She didn't
like it either, but in spite of this, she wanted it. It plumped up
when she sat in it, making her appear small. And all around her,
stacked on little shelves, were the books, the Oxford dictionaries
lined up, soldiers smugly guarding intellect. The carpet was
vacuumed on the bias, one stripe against the grain, one with, and
so the floor was like a lawn bowling green. She wore silk, nubbled
wool or both, and as we spoke, I imagined her legs crossing and
uncrossing. I squeezed a dollop of liquid detergent over the spore
growth in order to neutralize its acrid smell and asked, Are you
fine? My voice was pitched too high.

Well, she said, I'm okay. Hers was higher, a baby-doll voice.
I knew by the crackle of interference that she was calling me from
her cell phone, even though her land line was likely not more
than a metre away. Her little voice sang out, Are you still coming,
Alma? We'll meet in the ravine. I'll pack lunch.

The train to North Bay was scheduled to depart at eight-
thirty the next morning. I had yet to buy a couple of large tarps,
a nylon cord, a dome tent, Muskol, moleskin, calamine lotion,
Band-Aids, talcum powder, a travel soap dish, a bar of multi-
purpose soap (skin, hair, clothes), and a decent thermos. Lying
in a heap on the floor along with my enormous backpack were
my planting bags (a three-bag holster harness, orange and white
PVC-coated nylon, with suspender braces, holes punched into
the bottoms to let the root water run out), my D-handle shovel,
one foot bar ground off to lighten the tool (carpal tunnel
syndrome being a common occupational hazard), rain gear, a

supply of an Avon perfume product, non-toxic and reasonably good as mosquito defence, full protection Watkins bug dope lotion, a multi-season sleeping bag, and an air mattress, deflated.

I had packed a supply of men's cotton long-sleeved suit shirts, light in colour, several white T-shirts, an abundance of under-wear, cotton socks, wool socks, scarves, three rolls of top-quality duct tape, a weekend bra and a supply of tampons. The list of necessities sent around to the crew encouraged the wearing of rubber or rubberized gloves to protect the hands from bramble tears and other damage and from the seeping-in of tree-borne pesticides, but I did not have these. I never wore gloves. I could not feel the plant along my fingertips with them on.

I still had to finish sorting the biodegradable from the non- and wipe down the inside surface of the Inglis, the door of which stood open, propped by a large plastic Godzilla that I had once been given and which I had carted through various apartments, rooming houses, bad relationships. The refrigerator occasionally sputtered as the motor struggled to keep up to the warming coolant. I looked beyond it, through a little vinyl-clad window into the backyard, to my miniature Eden, and wondered at the crocuses, which had poked through the last April snow and opened their petals, presenting stamens to the bees already thrum-ming about them. I needed to rake the pin oak leaves out from the beds, prune, flay and bind the espaliered apple, stake the climbing tea rose. The box of hair dye beside the sink reminded me of my last task.

I'll be there in an hour, I said. I turned the tap on full and then slowed it down in turns, fast then slow, in the hope that the last wad of decay would break up and wash away. In the end I had to reach down and poke my thumb into it. I peered into a bag of black mission figs that I'd found in my fruit bowl. Little ebullient maggots wriggled in and out of them, white ridged worms, their reproductive fate sealed in the Baggie. Let us be grateful for their culinary demise. Others dine on nothing, shit, fast food. I told my mother.

How awful.

But, Mum! Come on. Black mission figs. C'est haute!

I don't know. Meet me, will you? she said. You'll be gone for so long, otherwise, and . . .

Yes, Mum, yes.

I took my mountain bike, my panniers and all my Canadian Tire money and raced. The store was full of people standing in my way, buying such trusty hardware items as Fudgeo cookies, disposable diapers and plastic laundry baskets advertised as Mother's Day gifts. I got caught up in the angst these situations often create. I became rankled; I was sweating in my armpits. My cart was overloaded but I threw one of those laundry baskets over top of it all just the same. A woman jostled me in the lineup.

Excuse me, miss. The woman was elderly, pinched about the mouth area; she had blue-rinsed hair. But I've only got one item, she said. Do you mind? I'm frail, you see. She held up her would-be purchase by way of explanation.

Oh for Christ's sake.

I waved her in front of me. She clutched a large transparent plastic bag that held a two-part kit, ready to be assembled at home. One part was a set of aluminum legs, the other the body of a pink plastic garden flamingo. I calmed myself by staring at a patch of hair, a coloured swirl of unnatural blue on the back of her head. Her eddying hair. It took almost two hours — the shops, the garden rot, the fetid leaves, the thorns. I was exhausted by the city, the expectations, these people moving in and out of importance and wanting, the smell of exhaust fume. Mother gave me a hug, and I was exhausted by this hug too. It was a hug that took, not gave.

Mum was down in the ravine alone, wearing white leather sneakers and looking lost. She wore the dusky pink of wealth;

she had studied the wealthy. Her skin matched this pink and offset it with the grey pallor of illness recently overcome. She was a person of former health, had declined in scale in such a way that in place of fat her wrinkled skin hung about her; illness brought on by drink and cigarettes. Her facial muscles shifted in a slow intense dance of concentration, she was searching for a thought. Words to fill silences. I could not bear her vulnerability, that flutter of sun-bleached pink glowing under the great maple trees. The park smelled of feces and we pretended it didn't, marvelled aloud at the blue sky and the sense of sap moving up toward the littlest branches. The trees had unfurled their new leaves, and the very air was tinged with the light green of new hope. If she died, I suddenly considered, I would be free. I was made bitter in her presence, and I did not entirely know why. We walked and walked and finally sat, watching the tennis players lob balls back and forth, our heads following the banal sway, finding comfort there. Mum handed me a now-cold grilled sandwich of roasted vegetables and a condiment of unbearable tastiness.

I've been wondering about trees, she said. How do the roots know to go down and the stem up? I thought you might know the answer.

I looked at her and saw myself. We were so alike, it was disturbing. We had the same small, upturned, schoolgirlish nose, the same smattering of dark freckles, the same perfectly arched eyebrows framing identical green, oval eyes. I was her doppelgänger, but decades younger. I thought of the hair dye at home and breathed a sigh of relief. I would not be like her; I would be fiercely not like her. The hair would only be the beginning.

I don't know, Mum, they just do, I said. But I did know. Roots had many properties: they anchored the growing plant, they sought water and minerals, they stored food safely away from most animals. The roots went down because that was their job, because they weren't stems, meristems, axillary buds, flowers, because the cotyledon halves of the seed had sent them there. I told her instead how treeplanters regularly laid their tree bundles in rows along the ground and hacked the bottom half of the roots away with their razor sharp shovels. This diminished the tree's strength, lessening its likelihood for survival but making it much easier to plant. The first time I encountered this practice, I was watching a veteran planter, a highballer, Karl, who reeked of garlic and had the rheumy eyes of a drinker. I saw him from a distance when he thought no one was looking. He picked up his shovel and drove it down like a man seeking revenge on the earth. Again and again.

I watched in dismay. What are you doing?

He looked at me, a snarl pulling his lip away from his teeth, and then he seemed to consciously settle this tic in order to smile. It doesn't bother them, he said. Well, only a little. It disenchants them. He spoke in a soft accent.

Disenchants? I said.

Yes, that's right. They don't know anymore where they are going.

I corrected him. Disorients them, then, you mean.

Yes, I mean that, actually. His long fingers were red with cold, his nails pale blue-pink moons set into them; the nails were bulbous, slightly larger than they ought proportionally to have been. He stuffed his hands into the front pockets of his jeans and stared at me in a way that left me shivering.

It makes them work harder. It makes them stronger in the end. Karl was jangling change in his pockets or keys or something. Spittle had formed in the corners of his lips.

Your accent, I said.

Karl's eyebrow rose fractionally, and I watched his eyes scan me, along my topography, tits, belly, the slight gape of cloth between my legs. He was memorizing.

I am not German, well, only very slightly, he said, though there are some who believe I have a linear claim to royalty. My father, he was five generations Canadian military, you see, he took me over there and raised me with the help of a sort of au pair. I kept the accent, can't shake it. I don't know a word of German anymore and my English is pretty much crap. I speak English in translation, like my au pair, and I do not know the original. I call it shadow English. I'm nothing really. Which is why, I suppose, I'm here in this hell at my age. You didn't think I enjoy it? Ha! I've been rich, of course, but I've also been poor like a church mouse. I just keep reinventing, you know?

What happened to your mother?

You've got gold in your eyes. I see my reflection there. Ah? He was staring at me.

Huh?

She's dead, he said. His eyes bored into me, through me, to the landscape behind. I began to move away. He held up a sapling, the slashed roots dripping runnels of muddied water, and he snapped it in two.

He smiled, said, Disoriented. There were signs of decay in his mouth.

There must have been disenchantment too, I considered. There must have. The trees were planted for future editions of *The New York Times* and first-grade toilet paper rolls, the pages of this book. The landscape was a devastation, a scarified abomination. Very few trees were left standing. It was a man-made tundra. Barren lands. Birch, alder and poplar stems stood in singlets where the greedy feller-buncher had passed them by for more valuable trees. Along the ground, where it wasn't swampy, where the water table hadn't risen when the severed trees failed to suck up water come spring, where it wasn't scraped, exposed sand or duff or clumps of gnarled root tangling up my shovel, it was blanched, bone-like leftovers — deadfall branches and whatever hopeful greenery managed to sprout out of that nothing.

Occasionally a grouse built a nest in amongst the tussock and screeched if I came near. Finding a plantable microsite could become frustrating. Blackflies rose light as air out of the decay.

I breathed them in through my nostrils and later sneezed or blew them out. They struggled against the mucus, not yet dead.

Gold, he said. Your eyes *are* flecked with gold.

I told Mum about Karl, doing his persuasive accent as best I could, describing his handlebar moustache, the renegade red bristles of it, recounting the tenuous claim he made as heir to the throne (fifth cousin, thrice removed, bastard child or some such ridiculous assertion) and his awkwardly roving hand, which had tried but failed to enter my pants one day in an elegant hotel room in Kapuskasing, model town of the north.

What did you do? she said.

He pushed me onto the bed. Alma, Alma, he cooed, I think I am in love with you. I told him to fuck off. I slapped him off me.

Mum gave me a sober look, though she was far from it. I'd seen her nip from her little steel flask; very pretty. She liked pretty things. The flask showed misty condensation around her fingers. She clasped it tightly, scared it might slip away and leave her with nothing at all. A whoop went up on the tennis court. The ball was too high, out of bounds. Mother offered the flask to me, and out of something, camaraderie, I poured her gin into me. I saw my mother's relief that I had not fully drained it.

Will you come for tea? she asked.

I will.

I dropped her home and then headed to my place, where I packed up the gift and a box of Peak Freans; she liked the assorteds, preferring out of these bourbon creams. We did not drink herbal tea.

Like drinking perfume, she said.

We drank Darjeeling made from civilized little bags. I dipped my cookie; she, never.

With that woman again, I suppose, she said.

I kept my mouth shut. To change the topic, I handed her the plastic laundry basket from Canadian Tire. I've brought you a Mother's Day gift. Happy Mother's Day or almost, Mum.

A basket case! How fitting, she said.

She lifted herself off the couch and brought the basket into the kitchen, where her stacked washer-dryer was hidden away in a cupboard. She opened and closed the fridge door several times. She returned and slumped into the feathers. I despise this couch, she said, flinging her tight little half-curled fist into it. Hate this whole apartment, you know. He's with that woman, I can feel it. I can feel it, I can, under my skin. Men are shits. She was moving into dangerous territory and I protested.

You know, I wish you wouldn't constantly target men. It isn't Dad's fault he's a jerk.

Whose fault is it then?

I don't know. You can't keep blaming him for everything, it's tiresome. He's predisposed; you should have seen it coming.

Blame the victim, sure. Cheating is genetic?

How should I know? I just wish you didn't have to slip it into everything, wish you'd get over yourself.

I am over myself.

My father, whom I love greatly and deeply, is a poor, sick, stupid man. He was an almost-soldier when they met, just eighteen at the end of the war, barely handed a uniform. It was devilish of my mother to run off with him. It was the first time he ran away and the last time she did. Canada was their land of milk and honey, not to mention ill-temper, high drama and messy divorce. What a spawn they found in me. A seething mixture of evasion and daydream. All the world could be explained away, couldn't it? Little diagrams of helices and enlarged DNA molecules wound in spirals around aluminum poles. Biologists could explain the want, the desire in vines to twine as they sought support, and they could draw pictures of what a leaf looked like at the code level. The mathematical beauty of this baffled and astounded me. But what astounded me more was that a tree, not so much in its sapling stage but in its prime, that canopy, the giant stage, so human that people

cared to save it from the chainsaw and built sleeping quarters in
its branches to ensure its longevity, that a tree was just a plant, like
a dandelion, a shaft of plantain, a stalk of nettle. That seemed
wonderful to me.

It's possible wanderlust is genetic, isn't it?

Roaming?

It's possible.

Running away?

There, there, I said. I wrapped her in a blanket and set her
feet in a warm Epsom salt bath. Her feet were like little bird
claws, so skinny, so poised.

I've never done anything to deserve this, she said. I haven't
done anything . . .

She soon fell into talking about my father, lambasting him and
praising him in turns. I offered her a drink so that she wouldn't
have to feel guilty about sneaking back and forth to the kitchen.
I poured one for myself too. I bypassed the drink she'd snuck into
the fridge earlier and grabbed the tonic behind it. The pong of
exotic cheeses gone too far hit me like a wall, reminding me of
the Inglis and all the work I still had at home. I dropped ice
cubes into the tumblers and listened to the background noise of
my mother recalling some ancient, unspeakable wrong my father
had perpetrated, a coat he bought for her, yes, the cheaper
version of what she wanted. Were we all in the state of becoming
our parents, of streaming into the sea of blind, wilful unknowing?
The notion terrified me, and with shameful relief I considered
I'd be on a train in twelve hours heading toward wilderness, away
from this other urban bewilderment.

Your fridge needs cleaning out, I said.

The inside of a fridge, she muttered. Yes. And then her eyes
fell upon the crossword beside her on the couch, the newspaper
folded over so only the blocked-up grid showed.

Oh, God, she said, don't leave me.

I'm sorry, Mum, I said. And then, You know, the roots? What

you asked about the roots? The roots are relatively lucky; they hide down there away from the view and brood, their heads stuck in the mud, while the rest of the plant, you know, what we really think of when we think tree or shrub or weed has to deal with the ugly scenery, the horrific weather and the annual Agent Orange sprayings.

They do that? she said.

There's bound to be disenchantment.

That's terrible, honey.

I imagined all my things waiting patiently, inanimate without me. I thought about the northern sky pressing down on me, the scent of clean air and the complex sensation of nothing for miles around. I said goodbye to my sleeping mother and, appearing calm, I left.

Chapter Six

So long, Mum. I watched the unfolding landscape from the window of my Via Rail car, the train reined in as we trundled out of the city over the oil-infused railway ties, past the old roundhouse. I saw GO trains filled with concerned white collars (managing all that had been made, all that irrevocable construct) from Whitby and Pickering, hurtling in beside us. I looked over, as we passed them, at the still-standing but decrepit red CNR cars, fading to orange, bleeding rust. Quickly the urbanscape gave way to an array of carefully positioned housing subdivisions, mile upon mile, a conundrum of suburbia, a landscape in which the forests had been hastily removed to make way for a progression of hideous and ever more hideous "homes," sod laid and then cut into natural-appearing curves, to make way for new, improved forests — the tidy, preconceived gardens of our civilized imaginations. And then these communities ended, and a new view unfurled — the scattered plywood, Ty-Veked, do-it-yourself cabins of the impoverished hopeful or the once-flush-but-now-worried unemployed. The Ty-Vek, or sometimes tarpaper, had begun to pull off, three or four surly hounds were chained to a single peeling particleboard kennel. These gardens had no sod, just trampled, self-sown clumps of crabgrass that may or may not hide slightly decayed dog shit. And then these hopeless abodes gave way to the odd trailer park, and then nothing, or rather nothing and then clusters of pink and white aluminum-sided Victorians minus the charm of stained glass and fancy brick, and amidst these, a little converted bungalow barely edible edibles — chips, candy bars, sticky artificially reddened cherries covered in chocolate and possibly housing, like the one I once to my fascination and dismay purchased, a small colony of fervent caffeinated ants hauling wads of goop out though a small chewed tear in the corner of the box.

Powassan, Matachewan, Manatouwadge, Kirkland Lake, Co-chrane, Moonbeam, Kapuskasing, Hawk Junction, Hornepayne, Timmins, South Porcupine, Swastika, Hearst. I knew something intimate about the water table, the density of the soil, the back ways of all these places now. I knew the particulars of four-square-inch land parcels, each on each, severed worms, the propensity for the propagation of insect life, the likelihood of a moose sighting and further not much. There were little stores (Jack and Jills), Husquavarna outlets selling chainsaws and snowmobiles and motor oil, subsistence craft stores filled with ingenious banana holders and corner-dadoed shelves jigsawed into familiar patterns. There were used-book stores filled with cheap Harlequins and even cheaper stray copies of Omar Khayyam, Salinger, and once a well-thumbed *Johnny Got His Gun*, which I bought for ten cents. I knew the awe-filled, beautiful sensation of looking at the skies up there, the cumulus packed flat and tight — imagined clouds, close, so close overhead.

I knew a little about the Indians, their wily tricks on us foolish colonials. Getting on the bus in North Bay, exhausted, I watched a family, an extended family, maybe twenty Cree board the bus — the Naugahyde sweat, the white plastic upholstery piping, the invigorating diesel fumes. They sat down chatting, then rose in pairs to move bags into the upper storage, shifting these same and then retrieving them. They hugged and patted heads in farewell. This whole operation extended well into the departure time, while the white driver waited patiently, nodding with some nostalgic recognition of familial love, the spirit of Indian-ness or what-have-you, and this smile twisted as he tried to comprehend the situation, as the family hugged again and went about their so-longs, climbing out of the bus and then back on with more parcels to stow and then, in turn, to unstow on the chrome shelf. Elders and children sat and then switched to perhaps more comfortable seats in a never-ending reconfiguration of replacement until all at once, the bus now twenty minutes off schedule, the entire lot disembarked, chattering, laughing, waving cans of just-cracked-open Coca-Cola, brown liquid spilling, laughter, as the bus steamed into gear, diesel spurt, and tooted a tired goodbye to all, to every single last one. I sank into my seat and watched the tree size dwindle incrementally as we drove north. The majestic acacia, oak, beech and maple forests around Toronto gave way to forests of dead coniferous stems standing in swampy lowlands and row-on-row plantations of spindly spruce. Ontario. It was familiar, a known place, unsurprising in its beauty and its squalor. It was, it had always been, and after a time I did not really mark it as important. It just was.

What woke me was the hiss of air brakes and the still, open air — that simultaneous smell of decay and milled wood permeating everything. I rubbed my eyes, ran my fingers through my hair by way of waking up. I was to meet the crew at the Hearst Motor Inn, but I was hours too early. I took a taxi from the station to town, hauled my gear into the motel, argued for ten minutes with the surly, obese, stringy-haired woman at the desk until she agreed to keep my gear until the crew arrived.

I ain't taking no responsibility fer lost er stolen items here, she called out as I walked away.

S'good.

I roamed along the highway and breathed in the resinous odour the sawmill gave off, marvelled at the sawdust mountains, which rose out of the earth like huge orange breasts, wondered at the orderliness of the stacks of two-by-fours and one-by-threes piled just so under corrugated rooftop shelters. Along the highway, out of the ditches, a few groggy blackflies were already emerging, and as I had not anointed myself with repellent, I was forced to keep walking, swinging my arms about me to spoil their feasting. I gave up wandering the streets of Hearst after a couple of rounds. It was a desolate place. I sat on a concrete curb in the paved, nearly bug-free parking lot of the motor inn to eat a soft ice cream cone (chocolate-vanilla twirl tasting of cold air and petroleum) purchased at the snack bar stationed at the lot's edge — a trailer on concrete blocks — and I waited.

Indoor-outdoor carpeting makes a damn fine mulch.

I squinted into the sun. A small, elderly man, tanned a deep, dirty brown, balding in patches, wearing a green felt vest, leaning out the driver's door, had backed his car into the lot and almost parked on my toes. I watched him go over to the trailer and buy a small fries that he doused with vinegar, salt and an ungodly quantity of ketchup. He called to me from across the lot, waving the box of fries about for emphasis.

You wouldn't mind if I sat down with you? A couple of potato strips cascaded to the starlings ready for them. He nestled his narrow ass beside me on the concrete slab.

May I?

The smell of vinegar had the not unpleasant effect of pulling the gumflesh up away from my front teeth. I helped myself. We spoke of gardening, a topic he seemed to know a lot about. He gestured to his rusted Honda Civic and the roll of grassy wall-to-wall carpeting sticking through the open hatch.

Remnants, he said. You cut it in long strips and lay it nice between the rows of beans and what-have-you. It's a beautiful thing. Nothing grows through that. Nothing at all. I get it for free from a place in the Kap. Installer name of Bruce. I can get you some if you like?

He had disappeared by the time Ortwin and the crew pulled up — three crummies and a white four-by-four truck filled with a dishevelled crew, the novices' skin swollen with its first taste of blackfly coagulant, the others, some of whom I recognized —

Karl, Joe and Ed, Clara — filthy, hair matted with sweat build-up, twigs, earth and bugs. They piled out, legs and legs and more legs, the endlessness of circus clowns. Some were quiet, some whooping for no clear reason, some stretching after the long ride to town. The horrendous sight gave me a sudden if fleeting sense of belonging.

Cliques did form in these large crews, gossip abounded, people came and went, friendship was transitory. This was the sort of job one was attracted to because it was not normal, did not presuppose social skills or the ability to function. It was a swirl of people, working apart together. There was no particular reason to make friends. It interfered with one's focus on making money. But for that first hour, I acted as if I didn't know this. I smiled, hugged. How are you? My God you look great! And I half meant it, not fully expecting the quick falling away of good temper in the field the next day, the facts returning as I slowly, bodily remembered them — the bugs, the cold, the rain, the heat, the bending, the money, the money, the money, the smell of mud, the crusting of clay beneath the fingernails. The memory of earlier times would seep back into me as the muscles in my body strained against that half-forgotten physicality, treeplanting.

Hey, freak show.

It was Joe and Ed in unison. They held my hair up on either side while Ortwin, the crew boss, took a Polaroid, his perfect biceps gleaming white from his cap-sleeve T-shirt. The picture came out swell. I was camouflaged, my hair just about the same chemical orange as the Chevy vans. A colour not found in nature.

The crew got rooms in the motor inn, raced to the laundromat with the week's crusted work clothing. Everyone milled about town for a few hours and then converged at the Hearst discotheque; it was the only game in town. The locals wore bleached-white blouses to make themselves gleam fluorescent blue under the strobe light. We laughed at them flitting about in their convoluted mating dances as if they were an ethnological TV show, as if we were somehow above the same behaviour. I was anxious and bored. I wanted to get to work, to get out in the field again.

Karl sat down on the bar stool beside me and patted my hand, told me how much he missed me, how this year he would show me his true colours, that love was often slow burning, and didn't I agree? I admit I may have led him on, that I smiled encouragingly, that I enjoyed watching him make a fool of himself. All actions have consequences. With the privilege of hindsight, I can now see that.

Your hair like spun straw, he whispered. Your skin the white of purity . . .

Chapter Seven

My skin was a boiling rash, prickling red and electric down my arms, amassing raised welts inside the various crevices of my body. It rose and erupted like a tiny range of active volcanoes. Scabs formed and I picked at them. The heat around my vulva and anus was so great I wondered if the nettle juice had entered there. The doctor in the Hearst Medical Clinic, situated on a dead-end street, was a giant Cree who loomed over me, peering querulously along the angry rash that had developed on the inside of my arms. It was a red of frightening hue, each little bump a pustule of infection. Some of these had burst and scabbed, giving my skin a topography that I thought would probably end in scars.

It isn't poison ivy, he said.

No, it isn't.

He was exasperated. He had fathomless brown eyes, like pits into which one might like to leap. I could tell he was worried. He brought his face in as if to smell me. His fingers ran lightly along the tips of the pimples.

I've never seen this before, he said. You can tell me. What is it?

I don't dare say, I said. Usually doctors don't believe you when you know what you have.

No, tell me.

It's stinging nettle rash. As nettle barbs worked their painful magic, I was experiencing a euphoric high from the surface heat.

Uh, nasty. Were you weeding your garden or something? He

held my hands out, inspecting my inner arms, my breasts and torso. I was covered in rash, sweeps of crimping skin, itch.

No. I was treeplanting.

Jesus. You need a good antihistamine and some codeine for sleeping, I guess.

Urtica dioica, stinging nettle, was said by the ancients to be a useful remedy against rheumatism: prepare a bed of nettle and sleep in it, a pointed illustration of the adage, "You've made your bed, now you must lie in it." It is older even than flax as a plant fibre. Nettle, net, knot, knit. The Dutch call it brandnetel, burning nettle, and that term more closely describes the sensation of its barb. The seemingly innocuous hairs along the stem enter the skin like minuscule wasps, each one depositing a drop of hellfire. A person with rheumatism wouldn't feel the dull pain of it anymore when the nettle rash took effect; perhaps that was where the healing claim originated. I lied to the honest doctor, whose hands wound around me like a warm, human crane, lifting me off the stainless steel gurney. I lied. I had not been treeplanting. I did not tell him how I sacrificed the afternoon to gathering the already surprisingly tall stalks of nettle, did not relay how I purposefully let it sting me along the arms and chest and stomach so that I could better know the sensation, so that I could better relate to the weaver girl. So that I could better weave the truth. I did not want him to inspect the wounds or consider what else might be wrong with me. Neither did I mention to the godlike MD what I only realized later, once my pants were up and the poison began its slow burning infiltration. That it was nettle I had also sat upon. The rash rose over the cheeks of my ass and down into my nether geography. The doctor wrote a prescription for a corticosteroid in neat, girlish handwriting.

Take care you smear it on whenever you get itchy, he said as he handed it to me.

Thank you. I hoped this medicine would work everywhere.

Packed in my rucksack were a few extras that I did not mention in my earlier listings. I had placed my dome tent away from the clamorous throng, the microcosmic world that was a treeplanting crew, placed it off along the bush where the bold squirrels used it as a slide, where the birds, as time went by, returned and sang and flitted about the roof, revealing themselves to me inside as rapid whirring shadows, and where, on less bug-infested evenings, I sat outside in hidden solitude and ran careful little experiments as to the nature of nettle — how to ret, scutch, card, spin and weave it. I had packed a spindle, a heavy plastic spindle-whorl, a pair of carding brushes and a collapsible bucket bought in Toronto at one of the outdoorsy stores that sprout like so much weed in any global city these days, the city breeding wilderness yearning or something. I had packed my simple backstrap loom. I hadn't had a proper floor loom since Evelyn was removed from the house and her belongings scattered amongst her family. She used to let me use hers because of the arthritis, its crippling effects having bent her knuckles in the most useless way.

Evelyn had been my upstairs neighbour until last winter, and upon my request she had run private weaving courses for me. She was brittle and laid up with a broken hip first on one side and then on the other. She had beautiful cerulean blue eyes set in a face of worldly wrinkles, as if she knew everything. She said I had a talent for gossamer. It was the end of an era when they came and took her and moved her out west. The apartment was left empty, and even when it fills with new people and their things, it will be bereft. It can take ages to miss someone who has become a habit. Evelyn always told little stories while I worked, mumbling them into my ear from the side and laughing at my creations. It was she who told me "The Nettle Spinner," and out of grief at losing her I began to investigate the possibility of making nettle thread, of making a panel shroud. I could hear her voice in it, and the joy of that gave solace. I thought I might go public with the finished thing, that I might make a gallery show of it, that I might achieve some success in this making of things. But in the end that wasn't it. I just wanted to hear her voice again, and that's why I started. I chose comfort.

Nettle stalks hung upside down to dry along the branches of a white pine just behind my tent. The stinging hairs had wilted and were no longer dangerous. The retting nettle in my bucket had begun to ferment and gave off a sweet fetid smell. I stirred it for a minute, the work releasing my muscles from the day's labour, letting my body feel whole again. I wished I knew what nettle should smell like, what it should feel like as it decayed. Unfortunately, very little information survived time. Nettle cloth was thought to be a fabric spun from a devil plant, an impossible product and therefore magical. The Germans, who profited from studies done in Sweden during World War I, set the peasant women to making it when the flax and cotton supplies dwindled during World War II. I imagined German weavers patriotically fabricating shirt after factory shirt of magical quality, thin and warm, soft as baby bottoms, frantically weaving undergarments for their fighting boys to protect them from the elements, from corruption, from certain death.

Three weeks passed. Food nauseated me. The rhythm of the day, the smell of the trees, the ineffable, inhospitable, clearcut surroundings combined to make me feel sick to my stomach. This was not uncommon. I was not the only one. I watched one other girl picking over her salad, skipping meals. The bush forced an anxious anorexia; the air was chaotic with blackflies, a frantic atmosphere made manifest. Sometimes all I could manage was a pancake or a piece of cold whole wheat toast in the morning. I lived on apples, Oreo cookies and water through the day. Dinner was my only hope to refurbish the screaming cells in my rapidly emaciating body. I ate salad if I could manage it.

All my energy, even the energy of cringing stomach wall as starvation shrank it by the hour, was focused on the next plantable microsite, the next tree, the next stoop, the next screef (toe waggling, shovel tearing, get that damn duff out of the way), the next small addition of gold to the coffer. I was settling into the adrenal routine of piecemeal capitalism. I made myself peripheral within the group and kept off to myself. I left the limelight to Joe and Ed, loggers from BC (whose five letters between them were more than they deserved in terms of intellect), their unabashed Van Halen riffs and their rugged Muskol-and-baby-oil-slathered au naturel prancings through the bush. I left it to the Rajneesh, Osho (his real name was Frank Meaken), whose lover was the camp cook, Marilene. He screamed *fuck* with each wielded shovel and *you* with each planted tree, so the day added up to hundreds of fuck . . . you, fuck . . . yous, a mantra of rebellion soothing only him. And to Paul, the Australian fatboy whose parentage was dubious (carnies? gypsies? both?) and who came all this way to lose a few pounds so his wife down under wouldn't leave him for the svelte bastard he thought she was probably entertaining even as he diminished. And to Clara, with her golden tresses and her face that looked as if no one had ever raised a voice to it in its livelong years, and to the myriad vegetarians and vegans with their righteous proselytizing, and to the meditators with their very composed serenity, and to the rest of the followers with their intentional poverty, and to Karl, dear not-sweet fifth-generation Canadian Karl, who couldn't let go of the family legacy, and, well, the list went on and on. It wasn't terribly difficult to remain apart. It would have been much harder work to feign eccentricity, and I needed my energy to earn.

Paul wobbled over to me each day after work, his smile wrapped coyly around a neurotic worry that I, a mere girl, had managed, through some devilry that no one, certainly no one here, could even begin to explain, had somehow outplanted him.

So, Alma, he said. How many did you plant today?

Oh, Paul, do we need to . . .

No, really. How many?

Uh, fifteen hundred.

His smile dipped fractionally and then opened even more broadly into a kind of grimace of painful horror.

Fifteen hundred, he said. Fifteen? How does she do that? I don't understand it.

He muttered to himself as he waddled away. Long, pale rust-blond curls bounced behind him so that he looked not unlike an overfed Renaissance judge, except for his clothes, which were a patchwork of ripped plaid insulated workshirts with taped mends. The beltline of treebags, latched over his expansive stomach, jutted out from his corpulent bottom, which jiggled in an off-beat fugal response to the jiggling of his belly. I watched him from the porch of my tent, watched him lilt down the incline toward the tent city, a jester on his way to the pavilions.

My rash had reacted quickly to the cortisone. The pustules were thoroughly scabbed over and had sunk into my skin. There was very little evidence except an oblong, a white patch along my otherwise tanned bicep where I kept fussing the scab open so it couldn't heal. I was horny. Treeplanting made me horny and so I fussed at my scab. Horniness was part of the descent to primalism that bush living encouraged, although the word descent seemed to presuppose that civilized repression was a higher form, a notion with which I was not altogether comfortable. The idea that sexuality was contained as if by the very flesh of each harbourer was ridiculous. It burbled up in the way we saw, the way we moved, the way we clothed ourselves. It was the hidden joy in every stimulation — the eroticism of reading, the eroticism of writing, the eroticism of eating, of drinking, dressing, undressing, bathing, doing a complicated mathematical problem, solving a puzzle, praying fervently, of dreaming, of cutting a diamond-shaped hole in the earth — the diamond itself an ancient symbol for fecundity — and sticking the root of a spruce sapling into it and performing this gesture over and over again each day. Well, that was my perspective — an edgy, growing, particular perspective — as my face bent down to that deed hundreds of times a day. I'm not saying it was wholesome, but I'm not saying it wasn't either. In reverse parlance, I had a terminal wide-on and it wasn't getting any better.

Waydeeho, Alma. Joe and Ed came up behind me and rubbed my ass. I wished it didn't get to me. I wished there was some disconnect between dislike and effect, but frankly they did get to me, the way they each took a cheek and softly rubbed it.

Stop that, will you?

We love you, Alma. They danced their tongues at me and planted away, laughing.

Clearly this was more difficult to hide than one might imagine. My horniness was an electric charge that built along the skin. This charge, either positive or negative, extended in waves or pulses out from my body and acted as a huge organic magnet attracting all manner of opposite charges. I was a walking electrical field. A sexual lodestone. Riff-raff began to smile at me; even Paul, bless his heart, wobbled over and gave me a hug one morning. A temp planter from England, some wilderness hack passing through, camped out in our bush camp and tried to smarm everyone with his baby blue VW bus, his fake posh accent. He stayed on for a week, looking over maps and trying.

I don't know if you've noticed, he said, but I'm rather fond of you.

Rather?

No. I said, "rather fond."

I hadn't noticed, really. That's very kind of you.

But you're not interested.

No, I said. No, rather not. No. Thank you.

He gave me a compass just before he got in the van and rattled off down the logging road, shouting, Go north if you change your mind, doll.

Doll?

He said he was heading for the pole. First VW camper van at the North Pole, that was the idea. It wasn't easy to be the first at anything anymore; the world was weary. I kept the damn compass, although it was broken all along. My conjecture was that was why he so unselfishly parted with it. It pointed perpetually north. Possibly this was a joke, the punch line to which I did not yet fully comprehend.

So people tried to engage me, but I'd decided not to join in. I'd decided to be apart. On the whole. You pay for that, being alone. Every choice had a cost. I sequestered myself inside my tent, jacking off when the urge won me over. Regularly. Otherwise, I sat outside and stared at the collapsible bucket in which the retting nettle formed a rich, pulpy mucus. It gave off such a stink I was concerned it had actually rotted. What a fully retted stalk looked like or smelled like, I didn't know. The literature was unclear. I knew that in various periods of Flemish history, there were edicts and fines posted banning the use of major rivers for the retting of flax and possibly nettle. This had to do with extensive manufacturing and the amount of stinking ferment the drinking water could bear. The peasants were forced to air-ret the plant stock when this banning occurred. Fog would have been prayed for, a good mist, rain. And after retting a man would come and scutch. I liked the word scutch and looked forward to scutching. It meant to remove the outer wood of the plant. The man who did this job was called a scutcher. I would attempt my own scutching. I would imagine myself to be such a person. I would infiltrate the character of scutcher and I would scutch. Then I could begin the real work — the carding, spinning, weaving and finally sewing together. As I worked one evening, poking at the mouldy junk in the bucket, keeping busy as a way to quell my tension, which had become feverish, Clara came quietly around my tent and surprised me so entirely I nearly jumped out of my skin, as jumpy as it was already. She appeared lost, in fact always appeared so. She was often found planting out of her boundary site, a sprig of wild camomile thrust up her nostril.

I hope I'm not, but I see I am, she said.

What's that? I felt as if she knew what I'd been up to only minutes before in my tent.

Disturbing you, she said.

Um, no, not at all, I said, trying to block the view to the pail and acting as if the stench was a normal part of my personal aura.

Word has got around, she said. I hope I'm not intruding but I heard through the grapevine, which may or may not be a reliable source of information . . .

What did she know, I wondered. I imagined a group of snickering day-off planters standing around a bar table, raising beers, the light from a strobe glancing off a disco ball while a dyed brunette, past expiry or not yet ripe, peeled away a few layers of her grub-brown Lycra bodywear to reveal a flat chest and card-table butt. No one would be watching, anyway. The crew would exchange little details collected over the years, admired, stored away in the recesses of their minds to be unwrapped and examined now, and all at once, too, as if disparity added up to truth. Details of alluring or innuendoed comments I had made in the past but could no longer remember making, accompanied by the clubby background pop tune "Hungry Like a Wolf," and any and all subtext to these were being pasted onto my obvious and burgeoning horniness. The wisecracking, its particular crassness, was beyond even my capacity for retelling. These were the sort of humiliations that all loners were subjected to, I reasoned. If you kept to yourself, you could be sure of gossip. I rebuffed Clara before she could finish her sentence.

It helps me plant faster, I said.

I can imagine it does. They say you are pretty good. That's what I came for. I was hoping you could do one for me? Clara's jeans waistband was rolled down to compensate for the weight that she'd lost in the last weeks. She had them belted Jethro-style with a piece of baler twine; a line of black hair travelled up to her navel.

Do one? I looked down at my hands, at the claw grip they had acquired, at the soil-etched calluses.

For me, she said. God, I need a lift. A story. Just a short one?

A story?

It was then I realized that what she hoped for was not a quick roll in the unnatural, plasticky, half-life-smelling nylon and polyvinyl environment of my dome. Word had, indeed, gone around, not that I was an insatiable orgasm addict, but that I told stories, or at least tried to once in a while, and that sometimes, if I drank too much on a night off, I might regale or whatever such a display of ego was called. Clara sat down and peered over my shoulder into the bucket of fermenting nettle.

Laundry? she asked.

Sort of.

I told her Rumpelstiltskin. I was rocking wildly back and forth toward the end of it and she was off in it too, her eyes closed and her lips turned up in smile. Looking at the soggy, hopeless mass of rotten nettle, I thought of little devilish Rumpelstiltskin and his insomniac spinning prowess, spinning gold out of straw, working himself up until he could do nothing but rant and dance all night in the forest glade. I read once that the word rumpelstiltskin was Old German for penis, and I ever after wondered whether it was really his *foot* that got caught in the floorboards when he stamped it so hard in rage. The original German version had him stamping his foot so his whole leg went into the ground and he pulled himself in two trying to extract it.

I had no idea that story was so sexually charged, Clara said when I finished.

All stories are, I said. Narrative is sexual. Everything is sexual.

For me at least. Lately. That's what I was thinking. I dreamt that night of the little Hearst man and me draped in some shining cloth, stigmata on my wrecked palms and on his lovely little brown arched feet. We stood on a rolled-out sheath of grass green indoor-outdoor carpeting, and the words *Patron Saint of Northern Ontario* echoed incessantly in my ears. I could not imagine whether this referred to him or me, and, to this day, I wish I knew.

Chapter Eight

❧ Burchard was such a wicked, miserly man
that for hundreds of years after he died everyone
in the land believed that rather than shoe his oxen,
he yoked serfs and made them, in their bare feet,
plow the fields. They called him Burchard the
Wolf. No peasant could marry without his consent,
so Guilbert the woodcutter sought permission to
marry Renelde. Burchard stood before the two of
them, smiling like a demented priest, not holding
forth but withholding.

We want to marry, Guilbert said. Renelde
seemed to shrink as he spoke. Burchard began to
laugh. For a time, he was overcome with giddiness.

If you can weave a wedding shift from nettle
thread, he said, when finally he settled the con-
vulsion, then I will let you marry, but only if you
weave a nettle shroud as well, for the day you marry
one another will be the day I die. Yes, it will be over
my dead body. And then he fell to laughing again,
a laughter that cut the sky. Renelde looked out over
the fields beyond his castle, saw the peasant weeders
rise and turn, cock their ears in the hope of hearsay
on the wind. Strong Burchard was made from iron;
he would never die.

She cried for days. No one believed it possible to
spin nettle. It hadn't been done in living memory.

But after the second day of weeping, on the morning of the third, Renelde's great-grandmother came forward out of her dark corner. The woman, so old she needed two canes, shuffled into the light, pulling her legs along with what strength she had stored in her hips. Her skin was ghostly white. Quietly, in her ancient voice, she said, But no one has ever tried to spin the nettle. Surely that does not make it impossible. There are nettles growing all along the ways and in thick patches in the graveyard. Let us gather them in. Perhaps something will come of it.

It took Renelde weeks to harvest the graveyard meadow. Welts rose on her forearms as she gathered the stalks. She worked surreptitiously at night, not wanting to arouse suspicion. She did not want to be seen attempting the impossible. She wanted the opportunity to fail without ridicule. Further, she did not want Burchard to find her and put a stop to her reaping. She needn't have taken the precaution. Burchard never ventured into the graveyard; he was terrified of death.

As she worked, Renelde discovered that handling the stems against the grain lessened the chance of being stung. She scurried back and forth through the night. She was exhausted, like the walking dead by day, gleaning behind the wheat harvesters, not for her own bread, see, but for Burchard's storehouse — even gleanings were not given freely in his domain.

Once the fibre had been prepared, Renelde sat down to spin. She spun at every opportunity, on the wheel in the cottage, with a drop spindle in the fields. Whenever she was not working, she was spinning. The drop spindle looked like a top as it whirled above its stone weight. She liked the way

the nettle came down like silk off the distaff and
spun up so shiny and fine. Renelde had a way
with the spindle. The long, perfect thread was
spider's work.

Throughout the winter, Jake regales me with tales about the
Titanic. Most of these stories involve trysts with rich matrons
intrigued by his foreign tongue. Jake brags that his accent gives
him special skills, but the truth is likely more obvious. I suspect
his ability to conjure himself, then melt away at will was sexually
alluring (not to mention convenient) for the ladies. I mean, the
reality was he hid behind draperies, or so he claims. Not entirely
sexy. I don't believe anything of it, anyhow. He must have stunk.
He certainly does now. In his favourite story, the one he tells
most often, and with most variation, he is succumbing to the
charms of an enormously fat lady when she is thrown out of her
berth by the first impact.

What thrust! she squeals, just before she slams into the
opposite wall and falls unconscious. Though his body hurts, he
wastes no time in grappling with the woman's leather valise,
locating a suitable outfit, finding an unmanned lifeboat and
curling himself up under the port plank seating, trying not to
breathe. He is unnoticed until his saviours are well out to sea,
too tired to throw him overboard. Or perhaps they don't have
the heart with all that death around them. At any rate, dressed
in a red silk empire-line gown, he tries to be manly and pick up
an oar, only to discover that his fat paramour has inadvertently
broken his arm, the hand of which had been inconveniently
attached, when she fell on it, to a particular orifice in her
corpulent anatomy. It is true his hand is slightly mangled — the
index and second fingers skew off to the left.

One night he is describing what exactly he was doing with
this woman when we hear wolves baying close by. They call in
small teams, an oddly compelling round of howling, which

begins to sound, as time passes and they don't let up, as if they are calling out to us by some essential name we did not know we had. The boy is still, which is a relief to me; he has explored variations on colic the whole day through and I am beyond exhaustion. In a vain attempt to frighten them away, Jake begins to howl back. His call has the opposite effect. They draw near and seem to surround the shack, their howls an aural entrapment. I fall asleep to their music, but when I wake up the next morning, I see Jake pressed into the wall, his eyes wide open. Obviously, he has not slept one wink. Outside the front door there are pad prints all around.

I am protecting you, he says. He speaks as if out of a dream, mine.

The boy?

Yes. The little baby. Sorry, my mistake, he says. You, of course, don't need my help.

Certainly not.

If it's true he survived the sinking of the *Titanic*, Jake's well into his nineties. He's incontinent, nearly blind, impotent. And yet he forages and hunts like an old pro. It's as if he needn't see at all. The small beasts find his gun sights and bare their hearts to him. I know I'll never starve while I'm with him. Every few weeks he vanishes for days, and I notice my wallet missing. He returns with snacks and, later in the spring, seed packets. I appreciate the snacks. During the pregnancy, there was no end to the cravings, and once the baby is born, the snacks fill a void, some existential lack I can't quite identify. He brings me potato chips. I'm hungry, dissatisfied, and the sourness of salt and vinegar is all that will suffice. I eat them until the vinegar works its way just beneath the pores of my skin, past the threshold of saturation; then, revolted with myself, I fling the empty bag away and vow never to repeat the performance.

Jake. Why do you buy this?

You like it. You like it.

But look at me. I'm a vulture.

Jake laughs mercilessly. I pull the balls of nettle out. The baby's wailing rises in pitch. The boy has found a frequency that resonates for me. It responds somehow to my potato-chip angst in such a way that I cannot really hear it — it is a part of me. I suspect this is the child's intent, that all babes seek to become their mothers and then, finding themselves incapable, seek to disengage. I actively encourage this separation.

Get him. Rock him, I say to Jake.

You're an unlikely mother. Jake looks at me as if I am dirty. He would have cast me out ages ago except he's lonely, and he feels responsible for the child. The boy reminds him of the one he has lately claimed to have left behind when he ran away, which is off-topic, forbidden. He told me this accidentally and won't elaborate. Why should I care? His history is only useful where I can exploit it. No, I'm not callous; I'm in a bind. I'm thankful Jake does my work for me, grateful even. Perhaps I will abandon the baby here with Jake and go home when the weaving is complete, when the story has unfolded. Let Jake's dream come to fruition, leave the boy here as a sort of gift. To show my gratitude. The boy is certainly a beautiful pink against Jake's hands. He likes him naked, finds it marvellous that he can be so clean, so pure. He's already taken off the boy's clothes, checked the diaper for wet, given him a little bark-stripped stick to chew on. Jake's clothes are rough canvas, and he looks like he emerged from the ground, a miner up from the mines, a cob borne of some carbuncled underground cavern.

You shouldn't let me touch him, he says, looking up at me.

You're the closest to decent we've got at the moment. Besides, I'm busy, I say. I've got the loom working. I'm so angry, but as the threads unwind from the clew, they seem to draw the rage slowly out of me. The patch I am working on and, for that matter, all the squares as they lie heaped upon one another are tight, nasty embodiments of this energy. Little furious things.

Sometimes in the night, when the child has finally ceased its mewling and fallen into whatever sort of reverie such a creature might experience, I pick the squares up and read them in the dim flicker of the candle. They are fantastic, as if made by the hands of another. I wonder at them, I do. I can see that beauty can come out of ugliness.

    ✿ Renelde wove the wedding dress first. It went quickly once the warp threads were in place; the grandmother assisted. She woke early and put the hut in order, stirred the embers and got a fire going, hung above it a cast iron pot filled with stew meat for dinner, added onions, apples, bread and hops beer. She swept the cold stone floor and set to work. Within weeks Renelde had woven, cut and sewn the cloth together. The dress was as thin as gauze. The old women said she looked like a butterfly in it. The day the grandmother rolled the hem, Renelde stood on a milking stool outside so that the old dear could see her own hand sewing, so dark was their hovel by day.

    Burchard charged up on his own horse, now cured, the slimy worm circle a little hairless scab on the flank of the gleaming black destrier. He had left Renelde alone for some time, and she vainly hoped she had seen the last of him, that he had softened to her request, that a sliver of kindness he did not in fact possess had perhaps opened toward a generosity of spirit. In reality, Burchard had been caught up with bureaucracy, the fighting of a small tax he deemed unfair, and this had made him all the more surly. He slid off the horse and stared wildly at her, she on the stool — they met eye to eye.

It's a nettle gown, she said, drawing out the
cloth with her arms and bending into a faint
curtsy. She liked the effect her words had upon
him.

You've only half-filled the task, he said, annoyed.
He reached out to take the dress at the neckline
and rip it down the front. It was so thin he could
easily do it, but Burchard stopped himself. He could
see her form beneath the material, and although he
longed to see her skin and the little blue tributaries
beneath her skin too, what he really wanted was to
push her further from her goal, and what he wanted
even more than that was for her to return his desire
and acquiesce to it. The old lady kept her eyes down,
kept her fingers working.

Burchard reached out to run his hand over
the nettle dress.

I could give you a silk gown, he whispered.
A silk gown embroidered with wondrous birds
and insects, the leaves and tendrils of vines winding along the fabric in exquisite patterns. He traced
a pattern with his finger along her body. I would
dress you as befits a queen if you would only listen
to my heart and come away from this hovel you
make home. A woodcutter's life compared to what
I offer? You are more foolish than even your youth
can excuse. Think of it. The finest silken garments
imported from China.

Renelde shook her head slowly. Burchard
scoffed and turned the horse homeward. But she
did think about it afterwards, after Burchard had
charged off, the turf flinging out of the earth, and
she set herself, over the next days, to washing out
and drying, sun bleaching, carding, and finally

spinning the almost blinding white nettle masses for the shroud, which he in his folly had demanded of her. The material would be far softer and finer than the stuff for the wedding shift, which now hung behind the door to her room, wrapped for protection in a blanket.

Chapter Nine

❋ The shroud would be made of bleached nettle thread, uncannily soft and bright, with a sober integrity. Renelde thought about the slick friction of silk upon her body, its cold allure evoked by the cold water. She did not know as she hummed quietly to herself, hands numb as she washed and rewashed the uncarded nettle, the chill running to bumps down her limbs and along the skin of her chest and stomach, did not know that Burchard had begun to cough, a shrill, brutal cough that resisted the draught of cognac he took nightly against illness. She did not know that deathly sickness fermented deep within his body, growing hourly.

Guilbert stopped by, smelling of woodchips and sweat and the moss that crept up the north side of each tree. He had a sack, the remnants of lunch, tied by a cord to his suspenders, and a clean sharpened axe hoisted over his shoulder. He held Renelde by the chin and kissed her lightly on the lips, and when she turned away so briefly and so subtly, he knew.

Burchard the Wolf has been to see you, then? Guilbert's chamois breeches were black along the thighs from rubbing his hands there. He rubbed

them even now. The tears welled up in her eyes,
and he understood these as only he might.

The poor girl, Guilbert thought. Would the
menace never leave her be? I have half a mind
. . . Guilbert finished his thought by heaving the
great splitting axe from his shoulder and swinging it a bit too wildly in the direction of the castle.

Think of my dead mother, Renelde pleaded.
Think of the countess and what will become of
her without her wolf to keep her. Please, Guilbert . . .

I can't be bothered at all. He's beyond understanding. Guilbert checked himself at a strange
glimmer of unspoken truth in his girl's eye.
Guilbert tried to see beyond it to what was hidden
there. And the look on his face unsettled her.

Do you suppose you are the only girl? he said
finally.

She had not considered that there were others.
She imagined them — a harem of sweet young
girls standing one after the other — each wearing
a dress more fantastic than the next; what cost?
The imaginary cloth fluttered like the moths from
which it was produced, up and down her arm,
reminding her of the bumps from the morning's
washing as they travelled wantonly down to her
belly.

Have you begun the shroud, my love?

I have, although I dislike the effort.

What?

There is a chill to it, Guilbert, that I do not
like at all.

He held her, then. Comforted Renelde.

Within days, the first inches of the shroud
completed but with only a hint of its narrative

in place, Burchard returned. His voice was wheezy,
his eyes full of sickening realization. He gestured
at the loom, at Renelde herself, and ordered her
to halt the work.

You are killing me, he said. Burchard's vocal
cords were almost silenced by the germ that
threatened to strangle him. His clothes were in
disarray, the collar of his shirt open and yellow
with the stains of his fever.

I am under your orders, sir, she said.

Witch! I beg of you, he said. Talking caused
him untold pain, and he clutched at his throat,
mortified by the searing misery. In the name of
God. What revenge is this?

Only for the sake of the countess would
Renelde stop. She left the work in place on the
loom and set herself to some other task. She went
to the garden patch and pulled up the plantain
for medicinal tinctures and the lamb's quarters
for soup, simultaneously weeding the sugar beets.
Time was not to be wasted. Guilbert found her
there when he came to call. He didn't like to see
her bent over the gardening. Surely the old women
were capable of this work? The girl should be at
her weaving. But when he heard her story, he
whirled her around to face him.

Has he permitted our marriage in that case?
he asked her.

She could not meet his gaze. He has refused
permission, she said.

Guilbert pulled her by the hand back to the
loom. It was the only solution, and let misery
beget misery. The man must be forced to consent.
Guilbert the woodcutter would see to it. He sat

beside her and, to while away the time, he sang
her a little song that his mother had taught him.
He sang it to the thump of the batten tamping
the threads into the forming cloth, for the sound
of weaving inspired nostalgia.

Jake's playing with the boy's penis. He's holding it down and then
letting it go. Up it springs! I shouldn't let him touch the child.
The boy is laughing, so Jake laughs and does it again. If he were
doing it with the baby's arm or ear, I wouldn't mind. The boy
pulls his feet to his chest and kicks them out again and again,
and so he sets himself in motion.

What's his name?

How should I know?

We will call him Moses, after my paternal great-grandfather.

We?

Jake is pressing down on the child's penis again and rocking
his face back and forth. Ha, ha, ha.

Will you stop that?

But he likes it.

And so do you, I suppose.

He bundles up the baby, cooing, Hello, Moses, your mother
will rob you of all pleasure, hello Mosie. And when all the clothes
are on and the child is hidden in a heap of rags, the boy draws
in all his face muscles, concentrates and shits. Off come the
clothes.

You see, he likes it. Mosie likes it, doesn't he? It works so good.

His chubby's full, I say. I warn.

He's a man.

Seriously . . .

But it's too late. The urine arcs out of him, a golden rainbow,
and sprays over Jake's chest. I don't like to admit this, but Jake's
humour reassures me. I can't help it. His optimism is compelling.
When he's done chuckling, he dresses the boy, takes him out to

the pit and props him up so he can watch. I follow. Jake removes
his jacket and rinses it in the water.

It's warm, he says when he first touches it. It isn't yet May and
so I know he's lying. It must be just above freezing.

I watch as he pulls each layer off, the gauzy undershirt more
holes than thread. His old body is sheathed in a leathery skin,
which hangs like useless batwings from the muscle and bone
beneath it. Dwindled in age. I am curious, though. His body is
not disgusting, as I expected it to be. It is simply him as he lifts
off the edge of the pit and, with a surprising athletic finesse,
plunges into that dead water. The turquoise surface opens to
swallow him. The boy squawks and holds his hands up as if to
catch Jake's leaping form.

When he comes up for air, Jake smiles broadly at me. Con-
spiratorially.

Who's the father? You can tell me, he says.

It's a toss-up.

Wizened eyebrow lifts.

Uh, change topic, I say.

Sure.

So, what does she look like, your *Titanic* lover?

Ha. Yes. Change topic, sure. My lover? She is immense. She
is titanic. Jake's eyes have brightened with nostalgia. He says, She
is two continents.

Yes, yes, Jake. And you are the divide, right?

Jake lifts himself out of the pool and wipes the water off his
skin, using his hand as a sort of spatula. Let me tell you my story,
he says. Maybe you'll tell me yours then. And he pulls on his
filthy clothes and squats down facing me, close, and begins.

I have only to run my finger up from her ankle, he says, hands
gesturing, and make a small tear in her stockings and already she
is ready for Jake. This lady is very unhappy, I think. The night
is still. Where is her husband? When you see her in the corridor,
on the deck here and there, you don't see her passion. She is like

a dead person all dressed up, talking from a dead mind. Nothing comes out. It is all talk of nothing. She pays me in food and drink. I don't need money; I have my pride. I touch her and she comes alive. I go to her for many nights — well, I was young, so young. Her husband is playing cards or billiards or drinking. There is no risk of detection. I am the master of hiding. I am the stowaway! I enter her and she is happy. I go away and there is not a trace. Jake waves his hands like a magician, all pretence.

The night was still? I say.

Nothing moving except my lady, back and forth. He holds up his bent fingers and smiles naughtily, so I hit him.

Jake?

Yes?

The wolves? Are you worried?

No.

Days later, Jake emerges from the forest behind the pit pool with a coil of something.

Mulch, he says, holding up the coil.

Hey! I say. It's you!

He is dragging a roll of slightly mouldy indoor-outdoor carpeting over to the garden plot. Standing in this place now, for the first time, I begin to see what he's done. Planted a narrow row of radish seeds and laid strips that he's cut from his carpet on both sides, banking the little furrows. It is the most unnatural thing I've ever seen, a marvel of industrial genius.

Do you vacuum these?

We don't have electricity.

It was a joke.

He hands me a shovel and I stare at it, the pong of spring earth suddenly hitting me straight in the heart. I turn toward the road, if you can still call it that with the encroachment it has undergone, the quagmire, the streamlets meandering through it, the lamb's quarters cracking it apart. The road out. And I recall, for I cannot see, the decline of man-made forest along its edge, the blocks of trees planted fifty years ago, then forty, thirty, becoming smaller and smaller, down to those Willem and I planted last year, some eight kilometres away. Forestry in perspective.

They were there, right now. The treeplanters' presence was almost tangible, a racing palpitation, channels of my body running in that direction. Would they look for me? Had they looked for me and, exhausting all possibility, given me up for dead? I asked myself these questions for the first time. I watch Jake carefully turn the soil, glimpses of earthworms flicking themselves back into the darkness, the primal, prototypical miner turning shit into gold.

I tie the boy onto my back in his bedsheet sling, grab seed packets from the hut. I hold my favourites up to Jake and he discourages me. Too early, needs soaking, striation. He lets me plant only lettuces, sunflowers and peas. I want to give planting all my concentration, but I can't help looking up from time to time to the little forest rustlings or the strange call of geese returning in lonely singlets, no V for them, these few diehards that won't join the rest down south in the city parks, and I squint down the old road that I came up so long before.

How long have you known? I say.

It was the chips reminded me. The salt and vinegar.

What happened to your car?

The car got eaten up by the road one day. If you walk down there you can still see it. Upside down or almost. It was pretty much dead anyway, though it came in handy. Had to haul that damn table for a solid mile. That kitchen table in the shack. Found it in the trash by the highway one day.

People'd throw out their own grandfather if he got too old, I say. But he doesn't get my rib.

This is my last good mulch you see here, he says. I have it stored in another, uh, shack back through there. He's pointing with his weird hand, so I have no idea if he means straight ahead or thirty degrees to the left.

There's been something at it, you see. He shows me. The edge of the carpet has streaks, marks along it.

Bear?

Why'd a bear be interested in that?

Smell?

Smells of oil, not food, he says and raises his eyebrows at me. For the first time, I see his eyes are blue, flecked with brown. He changes tack here, points out the mould. Smaller critters too, he says.

Microbes. Coming at us.

Jake's face breaks open. He says, Maybe they're coming for you. He pokes me on the shoulder, a bit too hard. But it's true, something is bugging me. With all the bending, the boy has become heavy on my back, so I shift him around in the carrier and pull him out. He begins to cry as soon as he sees me, either out of hunger, which is the rational concern, or out of sheer hatred, which is the irrational. I vow to myself to make a better effort.

Jake reaches out for the baby. You should try harder, he says.

This irritates me. I throw the child in his direction, toward him. It is calculated and I know Jake will catch him. I know it more deeply at that moment than I know anything. The baby hovers in the air as if he is made of wind and feathers. But Jake does not reach further to catch him and he falls and does not cry. And then he does cry, a great, earth-shattering howl of betrayal.

You didn't catch him.

No.

I meant you to.

I'm not really here. You forgot that.

Jake's already walking away in disgust. I've got the boy by now and am soothing him, lifting my shirt and helping him latch. He sucks and sucks and then lets go to sob his bottom lip into his mouth and to look at me with that ineffable sorrow. His eyes say only, Why? I slump on the moist ground, wondering why this child expects something other, wondering why he hasn't yet figured me out. As he sucks, I am depleted. There will be nothing left. If Jake can disappear at will, I will disappear against mine. Sucked into oblivion. The boy sucks to calm but I am still not calm.

What happened to the woman? I call. It's a cruel question.

Woman? Jake is planting carrots at the other end of the garden.

Your Titania?

Well, he says. Maybe she was eaten by sharks. Or by time and salt water. Or red herrings, I dunno. Jake is on to me. But I will draw him in; I will try and try.

And the effect?

Oh, her jewellery was recovered, he says. It's in a display case in a travelling archive.

I meant how did it affect you, I say, not what happened to the effects. Effect, affect. Fuck, you're so stupid.

Jake is repulsed by me, I realize. He is pointing and backing away from me. He almost falls and then catches himself. A low grunt comes out of his mouth and he gesticulates toward me as if I am somehow frightening him. This cannot be so. We have gardened together all morning. My throwing the boy was a provocation, a test, nothing more. Have I failed?

Jake yells now.

Run.

Run? I turn my head and see the massive grey creature sitting on its haunches, tail looped up between its legs, yawning as if bored or tired, then smiling, its long canines bared. A cloud of blackflies rises around me as if out of the earth and begins to hunt. Jake, I see, is tortured by them too; he twirls and runs his hands up behind his ears. Carnivorous angels. I am more afraid of these minuscule black teeth on wings than of the wolf. I cover the boy with my shirt and run to the safety of the shack. I hear

Jake barking behind me. The wolf stares at us, a pantomime put on for its pleasure. Flies have followed us into the house; I hear the wolf panting under the window, and then it is gone, returned to its pack, perhaps, beckoned by a call so far off, so high-pitched I am not able to hear it. I lean over the sink, there is a glare on the window. I press up against the glass. I cannot be sure but I think I see a form, the form of a man as a shadow just inside the edge of the woods. He makes no effort to hide. I think I see him lift his hand and I believe he waves at me. I am seeing things, perhaps. I shake my head to dislodge the sighting and look again. I see nothing but the faint memory of a shadow waving.

It was rabid, says Jake, when he can speak again. He's been panting, trying to catch his breath. I've never seen him so scared.

You can't know this.

Otherwise it wouldn't come so close.

Conjecture. Oh, my heart beats in fear.

I whisper, You left her to die, didn't you?

I am a harpy for asking this. But I wonder. It bears asking what a person is capable of, doesn't it? In light of the situation. I can only catch glimpses of imaginary water pressing in at the door, the far-off scuffling of gentlemen trying to escort the weaker sex onto the deck and dubious safety. I reason suddenly that I threw the baby up in the air to test this principle. What would Jake do for me if I were in need of protection? At best, he's a worrisome guardian. His age signifies not prowess of survival but something less. An ability to evaporate at any sign of trouble. And luck in the face of danger. But there is another reason I'm curious. I don't care what the answer is, for any answer is half lie. I want Jake to know I'm apt to think like this. That I've got his morality in the balance. That I'm watching his behaviour. I hope this tactic works, for by it I aim to give Jake a moral centre, for his own sake and my own.

I checked her pulse, he says. I put my ear on her chest. I heard nothing.

Above the roar of water? I laugh. I say, The sudden silence of the ship? You listened for her heartbeat? You're a liar.

I am a farmer. He's whimpering. I'm not buying it.

You don't much like the sight of blood, I say.

No. I am just a farmer.

How Edenic, I say. Was she pretty?

Jake is furious. I can see it in the way his body begins to camouflage against the brick yellow of the hut's kitchen wall. I won't let him go, though. I need him. I see that now.

He says, I wanted to settle down in the new country, that's all. I wanted only a piece of land in which to dig, to grow things, to harvest. I heard things about free land in Canada so I found a way. I risked everything.

Except being discovered. Answer true or false. He is looking at the floor, his head shaking disconsolately.

I could not risk detection. Then it would have been all for nothing.

I weigh this for a moment, pull my nipple away from the boy, whose suck has become more habit than need, whose eyelids are heavy, drunken, and whose body has already begun to slacken into sleep — a state so preferable to wakefulness in a baby it is a wonder babies bother to waken at all. I've made a little bed for him out of old blankets and scrap fur that Jake has amateurishly tanned. It still smells beastly. The baby himself always has a reek of dead animal about him, which one gets used to.

At the risk of being discovered, you abandoned your lover.

You misunderstand, he says. She was not my lover; I was hers.

Jake looks at me with such guilelessness, I am undone. I begin to laugh and wake up the baby. I mean really. Recall I've seen him naked. Jake has shrunk to a raisin, he is not five feet tall, and besides, I've *seen* him naked. It's a joke that even I cannot resist. Jake is soon laughing too, and with the laughter, he emerges out of the wall and into the room again. There, we are friends now. The baby cries and together we clear a spot on the floor. I move the thread balls and Jake pulls the bundle of blankets and fur over and settles the boy by rubbing his belly.

There's something more to tell, he says, quietly.

What?

The shack where I keep my mulch carpet. There's an intruder.

What do you mean? An animal, you mean.

Well, it's not a shack, really. It's an old dry mine shaft about a mile in the bush. It was a copper vein in my day. Nothing much, a private enterprise, only lasted a couple of years, but it's dry and it's a perfect storage place.

And there's been a what? A bear?

No. When I pulled the carpet out, I smelled ash. No bear. Man.

As I try to fall asleep that night, it occurs to me that I knew all along. That pong of alluring earth, the draw of the tree-planting clan toward itself like a communal magnet, offering only just barely that — it was false, a false lead. It was coming to get me, and my waiting was not illusory. I was not making it up as I went along. He was coming back.

Jake?

I call across the dark room, and my one word hangs there so long it becomes nebulous, changing form and meaning until his answer comes, and I no longer remember what I've been thinking.

Yes?

You would have made a good farmer.

Thank you. To tell the truth, I grew up in the city. Playing in the alleys between the houses with my friends. He's talking peripherally again, about nothing. He goes on talking, clearly talking to himself. My mind wanders. I am not much of a listener. I've almost fallen asleep but Jake keeps talking. I can barely hear him mumbling outside my room. He says, Something happened to you. There is darkness now.

What?

You had joy before, in the parking lot, where I met you. You could laugh. And it's true, I can recall joy.

What is the conduit for happiness? I say.

You just make it up. That's how I've always done it.

Chapter Ten

Karl was in the cookshack rubbing his hands together for warmth, the stink of filthy socks drying behind the woodstove. It was a cold wet evening proceeding from a cold rainy day. We smelled of chemicals and trees and mud. I was standing near him and he did not seem threatening to me. There were other people there. I don't remember who. We did not speak to one another, but I felt him looking at me every now and again. I saw his eyes returning to his hands, the tail end of an assessment. I had been standing there a long time, unable to heat up. I was unprepared for the rain that day and consequently was soaked to the bone, to the marrow, to the soul. My god, I was cold. Slowly, though, the thaw began and I looked about. The evening was upon me, the people who earlier huddled for warmth around the stove had dispersed. The few remaining played cards, wrote letters, hunched over their work, chatted, passed a joint slowly from one to the next. I was so tired, it was as if I were in a dream. I heard Karl say, I believe in absolutes. I am pragmatic.

An idealistic pragmatic?

I felt suddenly very young in his presence. Not in awe of him at all but sympathetic. I was sorry for him because I was young and he was not. He showed me a photograph of himself as a boy in some sort of uniform, and I sneered. It was my impression that he was wearing a Hitler Youth uniform but he wasn't. It was a Boy Scout uniform. He pointed out this fact. Then he said that it made no difference. He might just as well have been in the Hitler Youth.

He said, I was young and young people yearn to belong.

I can't relate to that, I said. I never wanted to belong.

That's why you are so lovely, he said, and briefly I fell for this line. I considered that he really was fond of me. I considered that he might have some integrity.

I clasped his shoulder and laughed, said, Oh Karl. He laughed too. We were laughing about the same thing and I thought how seductive kindness could be.

The shovel went in, the earthen hole gaped, the tree root was buried. A careless operation. In some spots, in little valleys in the otherwise mundane flatness of the landscape, there were still patches of snow. The shovel tinged frozen earth and the reverberation sent painful shocks up my forearm. I hoped that the MNR forester, the tree checker, would come by within a day or two and that the weather would remain static and the frost intact. If not, the ice would melt and I'd be accused of missing plantable microsites and forced to replant.

Listen up!

Ortwin, crew boss extraordinaire, was digging at a low spot in the ground. We were gathered around him for our prescribed re-indoctrination, weeks late and more or less designed to please the ministry guy who was standing off to the side, trying to keep his khakis clean and dry. He resembled an advertisement for an upscale men's clothier, right down to the vulnerable squint. Ortwin had his weekend clothes on for some reason — maybe to impress the ministry guy. His snug velour pantsuit showed swaths of wetness where he'd walked through dew-drenched grass. The ministry guy was definitely eyeing him. Ortwin became animated, demonstrating his planting skill as a dancer might a perfect plié.

The cardinal rules of treeplanting, Ortwin announced, Okay.

He rubbed his palm slowly down and down the root ball of a spruce, twiddling the root tips along his thumb and fingers.

One, he said. Never plant in sphagnum moss. Two. Never plant in bare soil. Three. Never plant in clay. And four. Never plant in a depression.

Osho muttered, I've been in a depression these long years. And we laughed. Osho looked around and smiled as if he hadn't meant the joke. He may not have. His black hair was tied back with a strip of cotton T-shirt, his eyes were glazed from the coffee beans and royal bee jelly he popped for focus and from the inner darkness that was his motivation. He nervously tapped the ground with his shovel. I heard him later that day, fuck you, fuck you. He couldn't contain his nervous energy. Osho planted like the wind, his technique a psychotic hurling of his nightly honed shovel blade. Hurl. Plant. Fuck you. Hurl. Plant. Fuck. Hurl. Plant. You. I stayed the hell out of his way.

After the field class, we went out and planted the same as we always had, each to his own. Got the trees in the ground straight enough, deep enough, good enough. The shovel went in, the earth opened, the tree root was shoved in, the boot pressed, the hole closed — rudimentary surgery. I had my own secluded tit of land, surrounded on three sides by a low, bushy natural forest and on the other by a massive slash heap piled up by a bulldozer driver as some rampaging joke; the rest of the land had been fashioned into a labyrinthine corridor system, calculated to stymie any hope of strategy for the planter. It would be impossible, I realized early on, to plant my land, trees spaced as per instruction six feet apart, without resorting to a crapshoot bag-up at the end. This would involve one or possibly two large, heavy bag-ups, and then a back-breaking climb with these trees over the mountainous slash heap. It was difficult to predict how many saplings would go into the final inner nib. It would be a lowballer day and a worrisome one too. The area reeked of bear, and the wind was blowing toward the forest. Only the raccoons would hear my screams.

Paul swore and waddled about on the other side of the heap. Clara was next over from him, and he was rightly concerned about that. Further off, I could hear Van Halen harmonies on the swift, warm wind, so I knew Joe and Ed were close. The blackflies had just come out. I wiped a rivulet of blood off my forehead and another from behind my ear. The bear stink made me adrenal. There would be rain today. I was bagging out faster than normal but it didn't much matter. I was losing so much time scaling that slash heap, the Christly jumble of thrown-away hardwood, fast-growing shrubbery, bramble and topsoil. Branches and heaved root systems shifted under me. I'd been wasting even more precious time listening to Paul as he slapped the trees against his rubber boots in an attempt to lighten the saturated roots. We met at the tree cache and he moaned about how Clara has been planting in his corridor, how he'd seen her wandering about, and how deserving he was of my sympathy since he was colour-blind and couldn't see the damn tickertape he'd tied to every freaking marker tree along the way and still he couldn't distinguish hers from his own and . . .

Why am I here anyway? he wailed. Why am I here? I might as well kill myself.

You can't earn as much money in Hell, I muttered.

Money? I'm earning $53.27 a day before camp costs. I earn about three hundred dollars a day back home. That's after taxes.

But it isn't about the money, is it?

Paul grabbed his midriff and jiggled it lovingly. He said, I could have had liposuction for less.

Isn't it about the planet, though?

The planet? The planet, he shouted. Two little scars, that's all it would have taken, two little tiny scars. One here. One here.

I could be home convalescing, keeping an eye on the wife. Instead I feel as if I'm the main character in an effing Kafka novel.

The wife?

Aw, feminist? Right, he said. Sure thing. Feck off. And then he wandered away, the trees in his bags shifting around his waist like a weird and ancient hula skirt.

So the bears were awake and groggy; there'd been a few sightings already. A native girl brought up in Ottawa by Chilean anthropologist watercolourists had a male black bear shadowing her for two days. She kept rushing out of her corridors, screaming. The bear was seen lumbering about along the scrub forest left by the feller-buncher, pacing back and forth, his nose high in the air, crinkled in a hyper-sniff. He couldn't get enough of her. She became convinced it was an ancient aboriginal myth come to life, some sort of spirit show. Ortwin calmed her down, got one of the other girls to suggest she use tampons instead of pads.

She was bitter. She said, Vagina dentata. Tell him that for me. Tell him I know my fucking mythology. But she went over to tampons, mumbling about flow, and the bear eventually laid off.

Patches of grass in my area were flattened by bears. As I bent to plant, my nose caught the lingering rank stink of bear fur. I sensed them watching me, noses high, scenting me out. I sang loud songs of shifting pitch, out of tune, in the hope of discouraging any interest in me. I knew it was unusual for a black bear to attack a human. They preferred berries and small insects found beneath logs and stones, the occasional river fish. But still. The new landscape must have been troubling — trees gone, swamps rising where the ground was previously dry, lakes forming where new plants failed to thrive, and these strange bipedal animals moving about putting little trees in the ground, marking the land with their own new stinks — what could it mean? I saw blurs of motion in the forest. These may have been in my imagination, but nevertheless, to scare predation away, I belted out an old Joplin tune about acquisition. I sang at the top of my lungs in a false Texan accent and it came out better than I anticipated.

The index and third fingers of my right hand were bound together with duct tape. This was to protect them from the gnarl of root one finds as one tucks a sapling into the soil — the enduring roots of felled trees, the part the lumber companies don't remove, for it is valueless. These roots had formed dense masses. They scraped at the hands that entered and exited the earth. The duct tape served, too, to strengthen my fingers into a little robotic dibble, very useful for the thrusting of baby trees into awaiting microsites. The rest of my hand was red, it'd sucked up the cold the earth offered this time of the year. My skin was creased with brown stains, which marked me long afterwards as some sort of gardener. Brown calluses ran along the joints of my fingers and through the top of my left palm, shovel hand. The blisters that rose there no longer caused me any grief, so far from the nerves were they. My shovel was worn down to the form of that hand, beautiful. It was noon and I had only six hundred trees in.

And Oh Lord won't ya buy me . . . I squeezed some water down my throat, pulled my pants down for a piss, swiped at the blackflies to keep them off me, then threw my bags over my shoulder and headed back for the tree cache. There was Paul sitting on a blanched, debarked log, eating.

So, he began, all cheery. It's hopeless, isn't it? This Clara. She wanders right into my path and, as sweet as pie, says, What are you doing in my corridor, Paul? So I say, Look, this is my area, I've tickertaped the whole piece in blue. She says, That's red, Paul, it's my red tape. What could I say? I knew what I wanted to say. But instead, well, I'm a nice guy, right? We decide to retape the plot right along, you know, right along her last line of trees, then she's supposed to plant in, fill up the back, and I'll do the front. Off we go, no troubles. Next thing, there she is wafting about at *this* tree cache. Clara, I say, what are you doing here? She admits it then. She says, It's possible I'm lost. I bagged out right over here. And guess what, Alma? You got it. I'm fucked, the MNR is going to make me replant. Again.

You look as if you've lost a bit of weight, Paul.

Thank you for mentioning it, he said. I'm much obliged.

When you get your figure back, you can always just quit.

A smile broke out along his face, making him younger, more compelling.

Quit? he said. I'm not a quitter.

No?

Oh no. I'm a complainer. Hey, by the way, Alma, how many trees have you planted so far?

Paul, I'm sure yours are planted better than mine.

I doubt that very much. I've been crewcutting the roots.

They will die, you know.

I don't need to hear that. Anyway, look on the bright side. We'll all die sooner or later. Won't we, now?

The wind had been slowly amassing clouds: wispy cirrus clouds built to ever denser cumulus clouds that darkened to create a roiling yellow-grey ceiling above us that finally began to spit and then pour rain down upon us. This suppressed the blackflies, which were hovering about my head, landing, crawling downward, trying to find an entry point into my boot, along the bottom of my pant leg. I had carefully tucked my trousers into my socks, but neither this nor the rain stopped the wily bastards from finding a crack and chewing at the skin on my ankles. I did not huddle away from the weather. I knew that would only exacerbate the cold chill. I slapped the moisture from twelve bundles of trees, three hundred in all, and shoved them into the two side bags. I sat on the bags to compress the trees and make enough room. I scarfed down a couple of cookies and picked my way over the slash. It'd be my last journey that day, although I did not know it at the time. I forgot to sing. I mulled over Paul and Clara, the idea of fairness, the idea of the body and its space, the diminishing return of weight loss. I meandered into concepts of morality and the planting of trees and wondered why wrong was so clearly defined but right so blurred. What was a crime? Why were certain behaviours wrong? Why did wrong linger and right evaporate? There was a connection between moral right and happiness that seemed superficial, as if good actions and joy were not as complex as bad actions and misery.

It was easy to look around at the heaps of ripped-up brush, at the forest floor trying to regenerate, at the lumber left behind and take the high ground. But that was crap and I knew it. I wasn't there for the ecosystem; this wasn't a system anymore. I was there for the money and the escape and they were what kept me. Sustainability, renewable resource, ecology were just words. They no longer had moral charge, meaning, hope, truth. It was a capitalistic merry-go-round, starting with my morning wipe and ending with this preposterous landscape. There was no high ground. We were all too smart for that.

The relentless repetition of the day made room in my mind for a reverie in which I experienced no conclusions but many forgettable epiphanies, and so, by the time I reached the centre of my land, my mind was truly lulled. I was contemplating the boxes on the front porches of all the houses in Toronto, the lines of blue plastic bins, on which was written Reduce, Reuse, Recycle, and how wholesome they made one feel, and so I did not immediately see and then did not really believe that before me snuffled a large black bear, her snout pulled back in a toothy sneer as she sniffed me out. The rain frayed my odour, and it took some time, my heart nearly arrested in anticipation, for the bear to figure out what I was. I reminded myself not to run. The words, My friends all drive Porsches, sprang to my mind and became a frantic refrain.

I must make amends, I must make amends.

There was very little for the animals to eat this early in the spring. There were common rules for behaviour around bears and for bear behaviour. I knew what to do. Knew what they would likely do. Black bears rarely attacked humans unless they were separated from their cubs. Even then, a female black bear might opt for the path of least resistance. It was highly unusual for a black bear to injure a human. But they did sometimes, if they were sick or mad or habituated to human presence or feeling insecure about this or that. I could always try to fight her off. The image almost made me laugh. I had almost twenty pounds of wet trees in the bags harnessed to me, so running away was a dangerous strategy. I had no time to think about tactics. I acted. I made to pounce on her, made myself as large and menacing as possible, growled and barked for all I was worth. If she came toward me, I planned to crumble and pretend to die. Perhaps I really would die from fright or what might be described later as an anomalous black bear mauling, a first in Ontario history, probably victim-incited. The she-bear would be tracked and destroyed, not out of malice or retribution but as a precaution. Well, it would be too late for that. I pulled out a couple of tree bundles to hurl at her but I needn't have. She turned and bounded away. I threw the trees anyway. There was no way I was going to plant in that area anymore. The MNR could fine me if they dared to pass the wall of bear stink and were lucky enough to find my throwaways and live to tell about it. I turned my bags over, dropped about two hundred saplings and walked out early.

Where you going? Paul yelled after me.

I'm a quitter, I said. I didn't bother to tell him about the bear. The animal wouldn't scale the slash pile. I kept walking. I walked out. The clouds had already begun to disperse and the sun shone still insipid rays upon us. The blackflies re-emerged in a frenzy of activity. The humidity incited them to procreate, turned them right on. I felt one crawling up my sleeve. What time was it? I looked down at my wrist to discover that I'd lost my watch. Fuck it. I passed Karl on my way out. He stopped planting and held his large fingers up in the air by way of waving.

He shouted, You should plant near me once, Alma.

I brushed against a shrub and the wound on my arm tore open. All of a sudden, I felt heartbreakingly lonely.

Desperation had set in. I was dying of loneliness in the cold, horrific north. Ortwin's exquisite arms became a fixation. His tight, flamboyantly coloured second-hand-store pantsuits, sewn out of velour, of course, made him ridiculous. They had tiny little fashion pockets detailed onto the back cheeks, and I couldn't fathom who might have worn them even when they were in style. The arms did not entirely compensate for such peculiarities. It didn't matter. I wasn't keen on *him*. I liked the disembodied fantasy, the beautiful arms floating in my lurid daydreams. I thought about them, the sinew of muscle sliding down the forearms, the tan youthful skin over the biceps, the curl of elbow that begged to be carved in marble by some talented long-dead sculptor. Evenings, I huddled in my sub-zero sleeping bag and pondered those arms, applying them to several scenarios the subject matter of which involved late-night affairs of unlikely acrobatics. Just the arms. I tried to diffuse the rising narrative of my imaginings, warning myself that I had other more im-portant, more controlled aspirations and that the last thing I needed or wanted was a scenario that might involve another flesh and blood person; anyhow, my fantasies were unrealistic. Ortwin was gay, not that that always meant anything, especially in the closed, clamped down, slim-pickin's treeplanting camp world, where musical tent was one of the favourite pastimes and pass the chlamydia another. But those arms were sweet; I imagined them wrapped around me. Not him, just them. My libido had completely gotten away from me.

And out there, the animals were ravenous. Moose had begun encroaching on the camp, looking for food to sustain milk for their newborns. They grazed the open camp field in small herds. Raccoons and groundhogs had dug holes beneath the larder of the cook tent, a large affair with prefabricated aluminum walls that hinged and fit together to form a stable structure made more stable by the circus-type roof — a grubby white PVC-coated canvas sheath that was pulled tightly over it and secured to the ground. The communal eating tent was attached to this, a half-cylinder lying on its side. We filled this tent at breakfast and dinner, our filthy bodies rising in a group stink — the smell of wet socks, Muskol, sweat, urine, trees and food rising to a pungent cacophony that we, after a time, did not notice. An ugly, dishevelled, odorific lot, we did not disturb the creatures under us. They came out at night and scraped holes in the plastic garbage cans when they couldn't topple them over to feed out of them. Emboldened after several weeks, they began to come out during the day, when we were away working. They stood outside the cook tent, rose on their haunches and chattered to Marilene, the cook, bored housewives looking for gossip, their children safely napping in the burrow. She shook her broom at them and they stood very still, looking up, watching her.

The animals were hungry. A single male moose was spotted ripping bark and licking sap from a birch tree. Its head was too large for its body, it had a small hump at the base of its neck, was likely infested with deer ticks and other parasites satiating their own cravings. The moose's coat was torn in patches from rubbing it against trees and from fights with other moose. And still it had a graceful ugliness, moving silently along its way like an ungainly dancer. I knew that the male moose, the bull, was relegated to one mating season — unlike me, who was frantic all the time. During the rut, it was advisable to avoid the spectacular view of a bull moose in open territory. The moose's pent-up sexual energy could prove dangerous to the small, less sexually balanced human. An encounter could mean instant death. And not the coveted little death. My jealousy toward the male's contained lust was unbounded. I was hungry and I was hungry.

I tried to lie completely still in my tent after dinner. I tried to contemplate the little Flemish cottage in the story, its adorable window boxes overflowing in my mind's eye with impatiens and sweet pea. I tried to think about weaving its charm. But I was finding it very difficult to concentrate. My own horny smell kept wafting past and disturbing the train of thought. My mind seemed capable only of violent rapes, the torturing of helpless peasants, the whinging betrayal of one body to another. Concentrate. Concentrate. Ortwin's arms glided along my ribs and over my stomach. Had Renelde somehow led Burchard on, flung her hair in a certain coquettish manner? Impossible. She was only twelve. This fairy tale, so obviously about control, was shifting out of mine. I tried to slow the thoughts down, but their silky, wet qualities created a reverse resistance. His hands, fingers slid into my crevice. They sank and prodded deeper, with perfect regularity. The story slipped away. The arms, the sleek, tanned, shapely skin of Ortwin's elbow, which, from my viewpoint, arched slightly and beautifully above me, motivating me to acquiesce and forget about . . . his index finger met my cervix and was gently caressing it. My back was bending up toward him; I grunted softly. My mouth was dry, the fluid needed elsewhere. And through this, I heard the distinct rustle of approaching danger. The rustle. Rustle. I was not alone. Someone was coming.

Alma? Are you there? he said.

My God, it was Ortwin himself. Yep, I said. Yeah, uh, I'm right here. I placed my hand over my abdomen and tried by sheer force of will to slow the waves of orgasm that threatened to break at any second.

I want to talk to you, he said. Can you talk now?

Give me five. Um, I'll, uh, meet you in the office. My voice was shrill. I stifled the telltale panting, clenched my abdomen and waited for the swish of footfall on grass to die away in the distance, and then I let go in a slow, soft moan.

Ortwin's office was a smaller Quonset-style tent rigged with electricity so he could keep his laptop computer juiced up. The tent had a small heater that ran when the generator was on. This barely kept off the night chill. Most days began with rain or the occasional freak snow flurry, but generally the weather had begun to warm up. When the sun emerged, the struggling plants raced against time, seemed to grow in a frenetic stop-action. Blossoming flowers — wild orchids and trilliums — peeled open and died all of a breath. Still, the evenings shut the world down again and food was hard for the larger animals to come by. The bears were becoming bolder. One had wandered into camp and slashed open a tent to get at a candy bar left inside. The females were especially hungry, their pregnant bodies craving satisfaction. I waited for the jerk of my contracting muscles to subside to a hum of neural pleasure. And I lay very still for a while enjoying that before I got up to go. I pulled my clothes on, slipped into my steel-toed boots and crossed the field to the office. I walked through the cluster of illuminated domes, so many paper-thin igloos in which the rest of the crew read or chatted or tried to avail themselves of nature as I had been doing. Ortwin smiled at me over the computer screen, which gave a radiant glow to his skin. His arms were covered in a thick-sleeved burnt-umber sweater fabricated from artificial wool.

I have a favour to ask you, he said. Would you do me a favour?

I suppose that depends, I said. I felt his finger briefly pulsing at my clitoris in some guilt response. Ortwin smiled at me as if he knew how weak I was.

He said, Blood is thick.

I felt my face flush and my ears heat up.

He continued, My nephew is coming to work here. I want someone to look after him for the first bit.

I'm relieved to hear that, I said. I really was.

Well, I want you to train him, to take him under your wing. I'll compensate you for your time.

Oh yeah? How much? I was back to earth.

For one week, a per diem of fifty dollars.

No matter what I plant, that's extra, then? I said.

For one week, maybe two. Ortwin stood up, crossed his arms over himself and grabbed the hem of his sweater. I stared at him, tried not to stare at him. He said, I am doing this as a favour to my brother, you see. The boy arrives tomorrow; his English is rudimentary. He is a bit special. His name is Willem.

Special? I focused on a strand of hair askew on his forehead.

Unhappy, he said.

What's so special about that?

It's hard to explain. He just doesn't fit in somehow. Ortwin pulled his sweater off over his head and rubbed his hands up and down his arms. They had a golden brilliance, shadows dancing along the sinews of his forearms. He smiled at me again and said, It's nothing obvious.

Willem was delivered to my corridor late in the afternoon. He was a ridiculously tall, skinny, morose boy with a shock of black hair and the facial skin of a man twice his age. It sagged in pockets under his eyes and formed a leathery wallet across his cheekbones, which were jutting. The clothes he wore were ripped and mended with thick silk embroidery thread and ripped again here and there on the mends, the threads crazy Frankenstein seams. He spoke English with a particular almost melodious lilt and tossed the words out in a garble of syntax; his sentences came out not back to front but in a heap, a mixture, a compost of intention. He was, at times, impossible to understand.

Hello, I ventured.

I'm fine, he said. I don't need helping.

Nothing obvious. Sure. I had hopelessly undervalued myself. I cursed my horny self for allowing me to consent to this.

Chapter Eleven

There was a letter from Mum I didn't want to talk about. My charge — big baby Willem — didn't notice anything was wrong. If he did, he didn't mention it. He was a boor because of this, I decided, even though I was pleased he hadn't seen or remarked upon the swollen skin around my eyes, their exceptional bloodshot quality. I showed him how to plant but left out certain helpful strategies because I was in a bad mood, because like most people I was selfish at heart. I learned the hard way. Why shouldn't he? Fact was, if he couldn't improve by mere observation, why should I feel responsible? Planting trees wasn't born in the blood, it was acquired. Willem dug holes in the ground as if his life depended on the survival of each and every tree. Commendable but foolhardy. I asked him questions about his life. His answers implied a level of misunderstanding.

You have brothers and sisters? I said.

Yes, I am trying, he said, eyebrows slanted in . . . something . . . concentration, maybe.

I asked if you have family.

I have two brothers, big ones, he said. I am the baby. And you? You are lonely?

He was down on his hands and knees, pulling a clump of sod away from a site. When the hole was made, he got back down and broke up the earth with his hands.

Give it air, he said, as he carefully tucked the tree into the hole. He stood up and brushed away the horde of blackflies that had settled on his forehead.

It is chaos here, he said, with these animals.

You should tuck your pants into your socks. I pointed at his feet and he looked there in apparent deep thought.

There is something wrong?

Willem bent over and pulled his pant leg up over his boot, then pulled his boot off. There were scores of suckling blackflies there, and little runnels of blood oozing down, dodging the bristle of black hair.

Uh, fuck, I said. You need better socks. What are these?

These are socks. His socks were ribbed and made of a shiny nylon material. They were bunched down around his ankles.

These are businessman socks, I said. You need thick, impenetrable wool work socks. Christ Almighty, will you look at that?

With my thumb, I ran the length of his calf, smearing a trail of insects under it. I took out an aerosol can of DEET and began to spray down his legs, around the cuff of his pants. I had a roll of duct tape in my planting bags and I unwound this and wrapped tape around the bottom of his pants. He watched me as a child might, in wonder, taking it in as if it were a lesson.

Be thanked, he said. You are very kind to me.

Ortwin didn't tell you what to bring? I stood over him swatting at the flies that hung in the air all about me.

He said there was maybe going to be something, some bugs, that's all. It is fine, Willem said. I am really good. Really, really. He squatted down and patted the soil all around the tree and then stood up again, took two calculated, equal steps, almost precisely six feet, long gangly legs bringing their own comedy to this effort, and cocked his face, searching out the optimum location for his next tree, even if it appeared he was seeking a distant shoreline. I laughed and inhaled several blackflies, which caught in my throat, causing me to rasp and cough.

You are funny? he said. Why?

Your system, I said, horking up little black carcasses and snot.

That is how we are planting trees where I am coming from. For hundreds of years and some are already still living. You think I am so fun?

It's just that it isn't particularly economical. You won't ever make any money at it that way.

Yes, seven cents is not much money for all that work I'm doing. I am thinking that Canada must be cheaper than Belgium for seven cents each tree.

I don't know. Is Belgium very expensive?

Yes, many, many taxes. Much?

The cost of living is very high here too, I said, and what I said bent in two directions and depressed me. Willem saw the pall of sorrow pass over my face; his eyebrows shifted but still he did not ask.

He said, It doesn't matter. I want to come and live in this big country where you can get lost and nobody comes to look for you. I will immigrate here one day, I will do it. You know, when I was a little boy I used to go for many walks alone in the forest, hitting sticks against the trees to make a nice noise and all the while talking to myself in English.

In English?

I thought it was the best language in the world. Very romantic to my ears. He waved his hands around his ears.

Willem looked down then at his treebags, grabbed a tree and held it up. Treeplanting is not so romantic, though, he said. I am wondering why they don't pay more for each tree.

You have to do it faster. You have to take less care. Do it good enough. That's all. Look. I cut a quick gash six feet from his spot and tossed a tree in, all in roughly ten seconds.

But they maybe will die then.

Yes, but some will live and that's what they count on — that some will live and not all. Look, I said, in the time you plant one tree, I plant ten. If nine of mine die, we're still even.

Strange.

Except I've earned more money than you have — ten times more.

They should pay to me ten times more for my one good tree than your nine dead ones.

They will never do it. It is a system based on waste; waste is factored in.

Not honest.

Willem's pants were safely taped up at the bottom but there were still frayed holes running horizontally along the knees and thighs; these had been patched here and there with embroidery thread and what appeared to be old flannel workshirts, but even these patches had begun to wear and in places were thoroughly ripped open as well. I pulled off pieces of tape and handed them one by one to him and he covered the entry points. In the end, the jeans were more duct tape than material. He sat down on a log then and pulled out a packet of Drum tobacco and a little cardboard cigarette paper dispenser on which was written *Rizla Automatique* and rolled with one hand the most cylindrical homemade cigarette I had ever seen. It was then that I noticed it. Willem was missing half his index finger and the fingernail joint of his next finger.

What happened?

I was cutting it off, he said. It was accidentally.

I hope so. How?

With a chainsaw. If I moved so or so, then I would have fallen on the saw and be cut in half. Instead, I cut these little pieces of me and so I can live. Everybody in the forest misses a finger or a toe. Not so nice, I think, but it is like that. Then he shoved the finger stumps into his nostrils so that it looked as if his fingers were fully embedded in his nose.

The forest? I said. What forest? What do you mean? You work in a forest?

He took his hand away from his nose. Yes, I am a Belgian woodcutter. I am working always in the forests around Belgium and Germany and Holland. He held the cigarette between his thumb and stumpy finger and he flicked it away in an arc.

Hey, wait. I thought you were Dutch.

Not so. I am Flemish.

The third son, I said. An honest Flemish woodcutter. Hmm. Of course. I was in for it, I knew. I looked over at his smouldering cigarette. I said, You're going to start a forest fire like that.

Overnight, the weather changed from cold squalls to desert heat. Mist hung over us for days while the earth sucked in the last moisture there was to be found in the air. The ground began to crack in places, baked by the wind and sun. The dry air by day, combined with freakish dry lightning storms by night, made the northern forests into a tinderbox. The fire marshal visited the block and demonstrated basic fire education, how to dig long, thin retaining trenches into the upper duff right down to the unignitable mineral soil and a foot or two wide to keep the fire, which travelled quietly, snake-like, underground, contained.

Each tree stash had a couple of regulation water tanks attached to harnesses; little ineffectual pumping hoses extended from each plastic tank. When bored or hot, Willem and I strapped them on and sprayed one another, the water droplets forming rainbows, cooling us. There were fires raging all around us, we heard, but we couldn't smell or see them, and so after the initial training period no one thought much about them, and except for the miserable fact of having to haul all that extra gear in — a daily chorus of grumbling quite apart from the unreal danger of death by fire, that rising meltdown of self — the horror was entirely beside the point.

When I saw one of Willem's rollies smouldering in the only patch of wet birch leaf mulch around, the last of last year's now-gone canopy, I went over to it and heeled it into the earth in order to extinguish its potential. He shrugged and smiled at me.

There's nothing to worry about here.

No, I said. But just in case.

As soon as the air dried and the atmosphere heated up, the bug problem dropped off. Our clothes dropped off too. I wore a thin T-shirt caked with weeks of Muskol, sweat and pesticidal slurry splashed on me by the sprawling root systems as I drew them out of my sacks. I discarded the suspenders from my planting bags and let the bags hang down, cinched tightly at my waist. My hips had developed massive calluses, a band of thick skin where the belt of the bags rubbed. We threw the fire gear down at the tree caches and bagged up, Willem smoking and neither of us saying much. We weren't expecting anything but the mundane, the grind of endless bending and, if we were lucky, the euphoria of mindless repetition. We weren't expecting fire.

Forest fires happened on television. The animals fled, wild-eyed. We would too if it happened. We would run in uncivilized terror, fearful of the encroachment of death as it hedged us into this man-made labyrinth. Animals were animals, not to be anthropomorphized; they weren't like us, of course. It was the other way around entirely, except we were smarter than they were, in a stupid sort of way. But there we'd be, running beside them, desperate for any escape, forgetting momentarily, in the heat of the situation, that we alone, of all the animals, had tamed fire.

Fire was beautiful. Campfires. We stared into them and found ourselves mesmerized. But because of the fire warning, they were forbidden, and so the nights were still and dark; sometimes people stayed up drinking and smoking pot in the cook tent, in the glow of battery operated flashlights or Coleman lanterns. I heard murmurs on the still air. They came to me as a soothing drone, the fabric of my overheating dome a barely safe barrier to their conversation. They spoke of nothing, I knew — they spoke of love, homeopathy, reflexology, god(s), Keats, and whether school was good or bad.

I was restless, exhausted from the extra work it took to get the trees into the ever hardening soil, frustrated with the death rate behind me as tree leaders went in yellow and brittle and seemed to burn by the end of the day into a dry, unfortunate brown. My arm was rattled, the muscles running up and down it were shocked and tender. I gasped in pain each time I jabbed the surface of the earth with my shovel, each time I had to use my body to swivel and grind the ground open just wide enough to cram the roots in. I was tired of the vespiaries which swarmed regularly out of dead wood or out of tiny holes in the ground itself, like some exhalation from Hell, to sting — the radiating poison pulsing beneath my skin. The blackflies ate us in the early mornings, giving way to fewer and fewer mosquitoes and larger blood-sucking creatures as the day heated up. They came and fed.

I felt like quitting but could not muster the energy to proceed on this thought. I was pathetic, trying desperately to ignore Willem's beseeching questions — What is it you are doing in that Toronto? What is it you are hating about me? — feeling annoyed with myself for selling out for fifty dollars a day in order to mind this overgrown baby, this seemingly retarded mythic woodcutter, who slowed me down in my work just enough to make me examine it and therefore hate it, as if only in the slowing down it became real. The relentlessness of the day refused to give way to meditation, to fleeting sensation, an incantational grunt of effort signifying slow prosperity. I looked around and all I saw was the bleak landscape with no way out. The extra fifty bucks did not compensate for the grief of dealing with Willem. I vowed to ignore him as best I could just as soon as he was fast enough and just as soon as he internalized the simple fire rule of putting out his damn cigarette. After that I would plant out of earshot — Why aren't you caring for the nature? What are you so happy smiling always about? There's nothing to be happy about, anyway. Smile. Smile. Smile. It never stops with you.

Was he flirting?

Fire started very slowly. Ignition was in no way an obvious event. It could take days for the ember of a hastily butted cigarette to light a large stick or catch on wet sod, eventually reaching threshold heat and combusting, racing, devouring, as they say, everything it met, until it ran out of fuel and, contented, died. The earth cooled, the animals returned, new life urged up in the wake of the destruction. Of course, certain forests relied on cataclysm for survival. In my tent, I took my mother's letter out of my backpack and unfolded it. I had read and reread it, sought between the lines, read tangentially. The letter itself was full of banalities, betraying my mother's willingness to suspend disbelief in the world alive around her, a conscious and unconscious purposeful inattention to truth. In it she outlined the prettiness of her crossword-filled days, but by the end it was obvious she was in her cups. In tiny letters the PS read: come home soon.

I was homesick, in a way. I was needy. My body hurt, I was stiff and tired, I was bug-eaten, I was horrifically in the moment and wanting respite. I heard Willem walk by my tent, whistling, and I put the letter away and was asleep.

A bear was sighted in the camp the next day nosing around at the garbage. Marilene came out of the kitchen, wiping her hands down the front of her apron, grease stains in two streaks along her small breasts and down her thighs. It was spaghetti night, she recalled, describing the bear as a large male — curious and fairly unscathed, therefore likely young. She was unnerved by the sighting but not traumatized. She told Osho that she hoped it would come back so she could take a photograph, hoped it would come back when she had her wits about her. Osho said she was crazy (man) and told her to move the garbage cans out of the cookshack so she wouldn't be trapped in there with it. He let Ortwin know that Marilene should have the camp rifle with her in case anything happened.

Marilene screamed at him. You aren't exactly copacetic, Osho.

Hey, he said and held his palms up submissively.

Paul gave Marilene a hug and said, There, there.

She wept, wheezing, I'm okay, I'm okay.

Ortwin stood up after dinner and told us all to keep food out of our tents and that the Ministry of Natural Resources was going to set a bear trap. I pictured a huge, jaw-like apparatus with massive teeth clutching a bear as it went through its agonizing death throes. But they brought in a humane trap — an immense circus affair, built out of steel, already rusted to burnt orange and baited with rotting meat and decaying kitchen leftovers. It was designed to trap a bear in order to make shooting it foolproof — nobody wanted to shoot at a moving target, especially not if he happened to miss first time round. The trap was put into place the next day behind the cookshack in the path the MNR figured the bear took to get from the forest to the garbage.

The forester wore a tidy beige workshirt, crisp cotton, pressed creases down the arms. They all dressed like that, clean, in vaguely military costume, like parcel couriers or unionized plumbers. The mere whiff of a forester raised the invisible hairs on my neck and down my spine. He threw the mauled garbage can into the trap too in the hope that the bear would be enticed by his own handiwork. But the bear stayed away, the stink of decomposing meat and mouldy vegetables carrying on the late spring air through the campsite like an anxiety that would not go away.

It was hot at night, hot by day. The sky had been blue-white and open for days; the blackflies were in hiding, but the horseflies and the deerflies, like miniature fighter planes, dive-bombed our heads. The only relief was the journey to and from the worksite. We sat half asleep in the orange crummies — large work vans rented from Hertz of the north and designed for the trashing we gave them. The chill morning air kept the windows shut. Karl sat in the back and ate whole cloves of garlic, not to ward off Satan, although he may have needed that precaution too, but to keep the bug life away. He burped loudly. Garlic, mingled with his toxic breath, permeated the closed space. Either Paul couldn't stand garlic or he couldn't stand to reminisce about creamy Caesar salad dressing. The stink was more than he could handle.

Oh for feck's sake. Stop the van and set the bastard out. The unmerciful stench of him. Paul was strange in his ever-slenderer body, as if it did not really belong to him.

It keeps the skin very clear, protested Karl. He peeled a clove between his forefinger and thumb and offered it to Paul. The ends of his fingers — they were disturbingly, perplexingly large.

Paul scowled, hunkered down in his seat with his hand over his nose. You're ruining the air quality for twelve people, for Christ's sake.

Karl sat up straight as if he suddenly realized something. He looked indignantly at Paul and said, I don't see that Christ has anything to do with it.

So you're a stinkin' born-again, are you?

Not born again, no. Only born once and not yesterday. He popped the clove into his cheek.

Idiot, said Paul.

Paul? I leaned out of my seat and craned around to him. Leave Karl alone, would you? It's hopeless, really. He's just eccentric.

Oh no. Karl was bellowing from the back of the van. There's no need to change me. I'm just fine like this. And I want to mention that I appreciate your standing up for me, Alma. I always knew you would come around to me one of these days.

Uh, no, Karl. Just trying to . . .

No, no, Alma, thank you, he said. He lunged out of his seat and brushed his face against mine, first one side then the other. It is inevitable, he muttered in my ear. Our paths are linked, wouldn't you say? The garlic odour oozed from his pores. He brushed his hand over my chest and up in such a way that no one else noticed, or if they did, it might seem accidental. He popped a clove of garlic between my lips and into my mouth. This taste of earth and bitterness caused me to salivate unwillingly; I spit the garlic at Karl, pushed past him and moved up one seat beside Willem, crossed my arms over my chest. Karl fell back. I could hear Paul intervening, yelling at him, haranguing him. I tried to ignore this.

Willem was quietly, carefully dabbing Watkins along the cuffs and around the collar of his shirt. The very few blackflies around all seemed to flock to his sweet, fresh Euro-blood. He had little scabby pocks, blackfly torment, all over his forehead, which had swollen, giving him the subtle nuance of a monstrosity. His hands were road maps of criss-crossing red tear lines, and his nails were cracked and black with earth. In short, he looked haggard and bewildered. He had a T-shirt lying in a heap in his lap that he would soon pull on over his head in a vain attempt to keep the flies off his neck. By day, in the field, he looked from far off like a lost nun wandering about post-apocalypse. When he bent and scratched at the earth, he appeared even more lost, lost so badly that he might be looking for clues, through some narrative written on the ground, to his *own* whereabouts. Clara sat beside Paul but stared openly at Willem as he medicated his shirt with bug dope.

I hear you have your own company, she said. That's quite interesting.

Willem didn't look up from what he was doing. He muttered, It's just regular, actually.

Clara batted her lashes and frowned at him but he didn't see it. His face was turned to his task. She looked over at me and caught me watching her.

What? she said.

What on earth brought us here together? We were snippets of people; who were we really? What separated us from each other? What made us *us*? Were we swatches, little throwaways of other people — a hand gesture here, a twist of the lip there

— genetic, some of it, but the rest? Were they just simply found objects, appropriated behaviours? I expected this was it. This was the crux of everything. I was my mother's acquiescence and my father's twitchy fear of settling at all. Oh, the list of influences was of infinite length, beginning from the start of time, the weaknesses and the strengths of my ancestors, these held in the code that was me and handed down until, like passed-on clothing, they became faded, brittle, moth-eaten, hardly worth wearing. I am nobody! Odysseus had shouted to the Cyclops as he returned home. There Penelope worked at her never-finished story tapestry, her unweaving, her lack of story in the face of his. I am nobody! he shouted with pride and vigorous manliness. He might as well have shouted, I am everyone. Each man is but a collage of all that came before. Hardly the stuff of a hero.

Chapter Twelve

I find a beautiful flapper-style dress in the heap of clothing Jake brought back from the Sally Ann. I've rummaged through the pile trying to find something pretty with which to patch my jeans and out pops this. It's bright red and covered with sequins. I hold it up to myself when he comes in the shack. I'm standing right in front of him. I brush myself up against his hand, through the scratch of fabric.

What's this, then? I say.

He actually takes a step back.

Hello, he says.

Remind you of anyone?

Ha ha.

This is . . .

Yes, he says, Salvation Army. When I went to town to buy scraps of clothes for insulating the floor of this shack, I saw this dress and I remembered everything. This is like the dress I was wearing on the lifeboat on the cold night of the sinking of the *Titanic*. The dress of the fat lady, whose smell was still on my fingers as I sat holding my broken arm and thinking about her last moments of bliss. Is this so bad, I thought, to die at such a peak? Maybe I did her a favour. I stood over the bin of dusty, mouldy clothes and I ran the dress through my hands in the direction of the sequins, like a cold cat I thought all of a sudden, and I realized, that is all that really happened to me in my whole life. That is my whole life. One night, maybe one minute of life on the *Titanic*. I am alive then, that's it. While the other men were rowing away from the tilting ship, I cradled my hand and the sweet smell was more powerful than the smell of the big ocean. After that and before is nothing. My childhood was getting ready for this moment, my life — the mining, the shack, the hiding — is all trying to forget it.

Why?

It is too big. I won't take responsibility for it. There are houses, I stay in the alley; there is society, I am outside; you throw the baby, I don't catch him.

No.

It is too late.

You shouted at the wolves when they came after me. You scared them away from me and the boy. You swam in the cold mine shaft.

Yes, I swim in dead water, hoping for rebirth.

Yes, but you are not dead. I'm scared I'm losing him. I need Jake. I need him engaged in my game. I say, You don't need rebirth. You're the most alive person I've ever met. You laugh. You do. You act. You are, really are.

Alma.

What?

I don't exist.

I'm talking to you. You do exist. You do.

I can evaporate. You made me up. I'm made-up. Take the dress; it is yours. I bought it for you. A gift. Something pretty. Now I'm going. So, goodbye . . .

Wait, Jake. Don't go. The day. When the wolves were at the door baying and you barked at them and you were scared. The bugs were crawling down your shirt and you ran to the shack and you said . . . you said you were not afraid. It was a lie. You were. And — follow me here, goddammit — fear is a manifestation of being alive. Deny this.

I deny this.

No. Proof. I want proof.

I was not afraid of wolves. I saw someone, a blur of someone.

A man watching?

A bad man . . .

A good man, I'm sure. It was Willem . . .

. . . waving.

Quickly, I pull my clothes off. Jake looks intently at me, concentrating to keep the frayed edges of his vision clean. I take the dress and pull it on over my head. The fusty stink of it catches in my throat. It is silk, I think, the slip beneath the sequin outer shell is, and clings like water, like what Jake said, a cold cat.

I'm wearing it, I say. Touch me.

He says, I'm old, I don't know. And so I take his hand with its strange curving fingers and I run it down my body and, when I am done and I let it go, it drops down by his side, swinging slightly. I take it again, I hold his fingers slightly apart and I run it down me again. I have not felt a mouse's stir of sexuality in the months since the baby was born. I have been a mere conduit for food to his greedy, selfish mouth. Jake stands there like a mannequin. That is fine. I don't care for old men. I like the feel of the gown, I like the feel of another warm body touching me. And I have a good imagination. I begin to have stirrings in my body I had forgotten about. I take his index finger and I draw a line over my breast and down into the double-u of my sex. His hand, I turn it around and use it to hold myself. I am just becoming thoroughly wet, the wet is surging through my body, the wet is accumulating and driving more wet forward.

Jake. I am gasping. I knew you would be useful to me. Then I hear it.

I hear another gasp, an almost inaudible sigh and something sliding along the wall of the shack. It is not me. It is not Jake. Jake stands stock-still and I stop and drop his hand. The cloth of the dress is stuck briefly in my cleft. I rush to the window and

I see him. It is him. I see him running, stooped like a robber, running back into the forest. Jake points and shakes his head. I hate him. I hate him. I would like to kill him.

Who is he? Jake asks. Is it a man? Who is he?

I almost tell. I catch myself in time. You are old, I say. And your eyes have become rather dim. You don't know. I'll tell you what I see. I see a scrawny bear lumbering off to the forest. It is a bear that has scented us, a bear that has become used to the salt of human food.

No, it's too thin to be a bear.

Yes. I say it, I yell. I say it and it is true. It won't be long, I say.

The baby has awoken and is gurgling in a way I know will escalate to air sucking and then wailing if I do not soon pick him up.

Jake.

I am here.

Thank you. I am glad you are here. Will you change the baby's diaper for me?

He unswaddles the boy and I see it. A bruise from his fall has formed along his buttocks and upper leg. Jake brings his face in close to inspect it, draws his finger along it. We share an unspoken remorse, Jake and I.

I name the baby Adam, which even I must admit is obvious, but I can't help it. Earth. I am finding it easier to think of the baby in this light, as if he sprang up like the lettuces that are doing just that in the garden. I joke with Jake that his early crop has an oily, trodden-on, indoor-outdoor aftertaste. These jokes take the form of an interior monologue, since Jake is gone. As soon as the garden was in, he got restless and left. I realize how much he looks after Adam, now that he's disappeared again. I'm resigned to accomplishing nothing at all.

I am nursing, changing, rocking, carting. Adam grows fat. And the weaving moves along by sheer force of will. Consequently, the weeds in the garden are taller than the seedlings. I'm afraid of the garden. It's too close to the forest, which has an ominous presence of late. The foliage on the trees has suddenly opened and the small ground cover plants are filling in the negative space. It is an impenetrable black wall of unplaceable, horrifying rustlings and perceived, or perhaps real, eyes watching my every move. I no longer hear the wolves, but something awaits me, at least, at most, in my mind's eye. I am anxious. The weaving calms me. This square has a spindle whorl hanging by a thread that runs around the panel like an unravelled clew. It has a chaos to it that projects my anxiety. For added security, I have locked the cabin door from the inside.

   🗡 Burchard's reprieve was short-lived. His throat closed almost mortally, his skin ran cold and hot without abatement as the fever raged and fell away. He made his house servants bear him to the hut on a litter. So weak was he that he could not walk, could barely speak.

You are my undoing, he murmured.

She did not look up from her work. She would have seen his limp form, half hanging from the bed, itself a sweat-wicked stench of sick and damp linen, his hand entreating her to stop. The skin was deathly pale, his dark essence visible beneath it. But she did not look up; she opened the warp threads and shot the bobbin through and tamp, tamp. The story of his death unfolded, slowly, certainly.

Take her, he commanded. His words were hardly audible through his wheezing. Take her and drown her.

The stones that Burchard's housemen tied

to her ankles were of a goodly size, small boulders,
unearthed for the purpose. The woodlice scuttled
out and dropped down and hid as the stones were
fitted to her. She looked like a great spindle of
thread still tied to its spindle-whorl as they hurled
her off a small bridge, where the Mormal stream
ran lustily in a bulge through the forest at a spot
where it was impossible to cross otherwise. She
was left for dead.

All Burchard's servants denied rigging the
knots in such a way that they might unravel as if
by magic and allow the prey to escape unscathed
from the fate assigned her. No man would admit
to this. Indeed the men vowed that they had each
personally inspected the other men's handiwork.
One of the men was a noted net-maker to the
count, hired annually for the river trout season,
and was apparently beyond reproach. Nevertheless
the bonds had untied; the girl surfaced only metres
from where she first sank.

Scaling the muddy bank proved a treacherous
ordeal, and by the end of her escape, not an orifice
was uncaked with soil; she found clay in her ears
days later. Renelde pushed as much water out of
her dress as she could, sliding her palms down her
figure. She wrung out the hem and then walked
home. No one saw any of this. She told the story
to her grandmother and it went out and spread
about as stories will. Renelde sat down, once she
had bathed and changed her clothing, and went at
the shroud now with fervency and determination;
her very life depended upon its speedy completion.
The ordeal had a positive turn — the clay had

refreshed her complexion and she looked more beautiful, more pure than ever.

It was the countess who finally put an end to it, who managed to extract from Burchard enough of the events and who sought on his behalf to stop the shroud manufacture. Once again, she beseeched Renelde in the name of Renelde's dead mother, in the name of God — the Father, the Son and the Holy Ghost, all three — swearing that she would use all the power at her disposal to convince Burchard to allow the betrothal to be sanctified by marriage.

In the inside pocket of my backpack, I have discovered the broken compass given to me by that itinerant Brit a lifetime ago. It is stuck at north. I use my Swiss Army knife to pry it open and find the problem. The pointer has become mired in grime around its pivot. Cleaned, the thing works perfectly. Now I know where I am, relative to where I used to be. This is helpful in a limited sort of way but I proceed along the ill-advised thought: better than nothing.

I've been going into the bush with it on little inconsequential journeys as a way to acclimatize myself to my creeping fear. I know something or someone is watching me. I know it profoundly and as surely as I know that all this could just as easily be paranoia. My aim is to get myself far enough that there'll be no turning back, and then I'll be obliged to find the mine shaft of which Jake has spoken. I'll be able to deduce from whatever I might find there who calls it home. I want to believe against all reason it's Willem. There may be a sign.

Adam has begun to sleep through most nights and I begin to feel myself again, or more precisely, I begin to feel a reasonable facsimile of myself returning. I know I will never be the same, and this knowledge bends two ways. On the one hand I lament the passage of time, the loss of the bower of childhood I may never have properly experienced. On the other hand, I have come to witness a strength in myself I did not previously recognize, the strength that comes from accepting that all one can reasonably expect from life is a series of fragmented episodes, the ephemera of experience. When I'm finished the story cloth, I intend to sew it together, not into a fabric book, which would make some sense, but into a quilt, a running tableau, a tragicomic. When I hold the cloth up to the window, I can see right through it.

It has been many days since Jake left and I have truly begun to fear for him. I make up stories about what has become of him. I imagine I hear muffled screams dying on the breeze, imagine his little shrivelled body half buried under leaves and the aimless, lazy attempts of the murderer to hide him. Who would look for him? A final, perfect disappearance. All this indicates that I have grown attached to Jake. I have begun to recall — relive, I might say if I were sentimental — moments of our time together as if they are snapshots or little, lovingly edited film shorts. I see him swimming again. I watch his wrinkled body transform under the toxic dead liquid of the mine pit into that of a smooth brown prince. If I weren't so starved for company and sex, so impatient with waiting for the impossible, so newly rejuvenated with sleep, so reborn into my own body, I would say I was in love with Jake. This is absurd, of course, but how easy it is to be attracted to a man you imagine to be dead. It requires almost no skill whatever.

I've been walking deeper into the underbrush, day by day, letting myself get utterly lost in the infinity of root and shrub and tree. I walk away from civilization, away from the static array of planted forests behind me and into the tangle of old growth, however meagre and spindly it is this far north. I sink at times into little swamps and come across the scat and nests of forest creatures. I hear them run for their lives. I sense their fear and am in turn afraid. Am I, too, afraid of me? I am afraid of the smell of their fear. Yet I continue because I must find the thing I seek. I've been at it for more than a week, making furtive and ever longer forays into the dense bush. Adam is strapped onto me. He has become a settled baby. His eyes are wide open as if to drink in the very atmosphere. He smiles unexpectedly, for reasons beyond my capacity to understand. He likes the light play in the forest and makes pleasant noises. I wish Willem could see him, wish for there to be some identification. Adam looks around and is content.

I've had almost nothing to eat of late. A stew Jake made before he left has gone rancid, and I've been eating comfrey out of the garden. I go in and out quickly, more truly afraid of this garden than the bush; someone else is eating out of it, I've noticed. There are little cylindrical pipe holes where once grew carrots and the lettuce has been picked through. Someone has pinched the tiny suckers off the tomato plants. I take solace in the thought that Jake is sneaking back for food. But sneaking back from where?

Today as I meander through vines, pushing them aside without seeing them, I keep my eyes on the compass, which finds me heading further north. I imagine a new scenario. Jake is living in the mine shaft. He has disappeared again and this time from me. He has a quaint little set-up in the mine, complete with a kerosene lamp. I see him sitting calmly of an evening, pleased to have me out of his hair, away from my obvious manipulations. He thinks, How frightful that girl was, how difficult. He sighs in a pleasant way that indicates how much more room he has in his head, his heart, his den, his underground alleyway, now that he is alone. Tears begin to stream down my cheeks. I can't help it, I'm that lonely and desperate. And it is with this manifestation of my imagined grief so evident on my face that I literally trip over him. Jake is sitting reading a newspaper, a recent national newspaper. He is sitting in what looks like an old rotten dugout canoe and is much surprised to discover me so far from home.

Oh-ho, he says. Do you like my boat?

I had you dead, or run away, I say. I hold my hand above my eyes, ostensibly to block out the sun, really to hide my tears.

I paddled it by land. It is a land canoe.

Then I realize, as if reality can be simply plucked out of thin air, that I have come very close indeed. The mine shaft must be right here, and I begin, in a squint, to scan the area.

Paddled from where? I say. Where is the mine shaft, Jake? Where is it?

It is under surveillance, he says.

Really?

Right now, it's empty.

He folds the paper nicely and tucks it into his jacket. As we speak, the mosquitoes hover about us. I have covered Adam and slathered myself in chemical protection. Jake has discovered the art of walking through them as if they are a parting sea. In this he is Biblical. He brings me to where I most wish to go, to the place of which I am most frightened. It is a small slanted square opening in the side of a hillock of earth, large enough for a single man, a small dragon, or a cart of precious or semi-precious metal. A rude door on corroded hinges covers the opening. There is a pole with a tattered black flag of cotton tied to it.

This belongs to me. It is my prospector's flag.

Very official, I say. I miss Willem. A pang hits me. I want to enact the return of the honest woodcutter.

By yanking on a rope handle, Jake heaves the door open, and as I peer into the gape, I am aware only of darkness, of the shadow of the great earth upon itself. I can smell something frightful and I back away out of instinct.

Go in, go in, Jake says. He hands me a flashlight and his long gutting knife by way of reassurance and I take these. The knife I tuck into the back of my jeans. The flashlight I point into the hole.

That smell, I say.

I've hung garlic. Just in case.

Garlic?

It's crazy but just the same. The voice of my dead mother is persistent on this point.

You hear voices?

Go. Jake pats my back supportively.

He hears his dead mother. Can we never rid ourselves? Jake pulls the harness from my shoulders and takes the baby off me. Adam's eyes are sudden pools of meaning. He knows everything. I wish I could recognize him. Wish I knew what bits and pieces formed him. Wish by that knowledge I could feel he was rightfully mine and not something forced recklessly upon me. I go in, swinging the light back and forth in an attempt at understanding. I'm on my hands and knees, for god's sake. Water leaks along the walls and I see no sign of life, nor copper. Nothing. It is only a tunnel into the bottom of the earth, housing nothing and nobody. Willem is imagined, Jake is imagined, my whole life is nothing but a fabrication. The smell of garlic, the smell of metal and earth and lingering sweat, or am I imagining this too? How long will the reek of man hang in the air once industry is abandoned? And then I spot it. I am probably two hundred metres into this rabbit hole. I sense the hole closing, and indeed when I look behind me I know I have turned an ungodly corner, for there is no longer any light of day. I hear nothing now but the motion of blood thickening inside my ear. I am as if buried. Carelessly, lazily, by some uncounted murderer. I have fully projected. I reach for the object of my desire. It is a book. The cover is off, lost to time, the pages are damp and illegible. Water and insects have eaten away its meaning.

Who's here? I whisper.

There is a scratching that, even as I hear it, seems a pretence of fear. I begin to back out, unable to find the space to turn around. Deep in the earth, I think I hear a collapse. The tunnels are falling in. It sounds like a monstrous yawn. The earth is bored. There is no light. Jake has thrown the door over the opening. I try to kick it open but this is useless. Behind me, I hear Adam gasping for air in between wails of abandonment. Jake is laughing. He jumps up and down a few times on the door, laughing, crazy laughing. He is beside himself. Then, the door opens and a shaft of light shimmers against little particles of quartz I had not previously noticed, embedded in the wall of the tunnel.

You are born, he says.

Why the fuck did you do that?

A breech birth, he says. Ass first.

Fuck. Really.

But didn't you see it? he says. The old book?

I saw nothing with my eyes that see, I say.

And do you know what was written in it?

Nothing. Nothing written in nothing.

Oh yes, something. You had to flip through and read it carefully. We are being watched. Everything is being noted.

Jake, you're blind. The tunnel is empty, nada.

Don't believe. Let Jake believe it for you.

He hands me back the boy, whose wails have thinned to exhausted whimpers, whose eyes are dropping shut. He hands me Adam, and he smiles at me. I have company again. I think about the book as we walk back to the shack. I think about not thinking about the book. I am afraid of what is written there, for it can spell only disaster. I have it tucked into my pants, can feel the edge of the pages rubbing at the upper line of my pubic hair. If I destroy this artifact, will it still be real?

May 31. Watching her prance off into the bush was the most beautiful thing I'd ever seen. Her ass swayed like a glossy-coated mare's, back and forth. I thought I was going to explode. I thought my hard-on was going to rip my pants open. Just her perfect, round cheeks shifting back and forth and me knowing my seed was therein. I've loved her for a long time. I didn't recognize it as love at first that's how hopelessly out of touch I am with myself. I thought I was sick and I actually had physical signs, intestinal cramps which I thought might be giardia. Beaver fever all right. I let my eyes travel up her body from her lovely snatch, the line is sublime. It's like a fantastic vertical landscape. I would plant my trees all over her.

Chapter Thirteen

My spinning had not gone well; the plants I collected were immature, the cellulose fibres were short. The product seemed to card up decently, but the spinning was disastrous. The threads were weak, lacking integrity. I couldn't make a thin thread without it breaking and I didn't want a thick thread. I began over again, harvesting what seemed this time to be large enough nettle stalks for my purpose. The plants were about a metre high and the reaping of them was arduous. I kept a knife with me and reaped while waiting for Willem to catch up; the crew was on a four-and-one cycle and so, for me, it was four days of planting, one of reaping. I harvested along the logging road to and from camp, pulling nettle wherever I saw it. I couldn't hide the project anymore. Everyone knew what I was up to; everyone was too profoundly exhausted to care.

I kept my shirtsleeves down to avoid contact with the barbs. I still had shadowy white webbed scars up my arms and over the soft tissue of my belly and chest. One small patch refused to heal over so I bandaged it, salving it with calendula ointment that Clara lent me. I took comfort in the fact that the pus was clear. Each day after planting I gathered a small bale of fresh nettle and placed it under a seat in the crummy. My pail was too small, so I borrowed a few industrial-sized plastic buckets from the cook tent.

You look tired, I said to Marilene. Her chest was shrunken under her apron; her eyes were wide raccoon eyes, rimmed with sleeplessness.

It's the bear. I can't sleep.

Really? You hear it?

Actually it's not the bear exactly. It's Osho's fear of the bear. He's tossing and turning. He's paranoid the bear is after me, that it'll get between us.

An irrational fear of death, I said.

He sweats all night; he can't meditate. She put her hands up and touched her fingers to her thumbs in feigned supplication, little zeros held up to the gods.

Ah, I said, an irrational fear of inner harmony.

Marilene smiled.

It was around that time that out of boredom I began to tell Willem more about the Nettle Spinner. I give him only enough to whet his appetite, keeping my resolve to dispense the story in pieces and so save the whole for myself. I described to him the little cottage of my dreams in French Flanders, the blue gingham curtains fluttering, a warm spring breeze enticing me to push open the tiny leaded windows and air out the place. I told him about the chinking needed to seal the north wall from the insipid humidity of winter in Europe. I was convincing.

I have an extra wood stove. You can have it, he said.

Thank you. The house is near La Quesnoy.

Nice, he said. Why not give me the telephone number?

No, I don't have a telephone. In fact, I've never actually been there.

But the curtains? he said.

It's just a story.

Willem pushed me and I tripped over a tray of container stock trees, barely caught myself from falling by grabbing onto his arm. I shoved him by way of repayment and we tussled for a bit, laughing.

Crazy-girl.

Hey!

He planted faster now but still refused to lower his personal standards. I outplanted him by double. He yelled at me when he came across a leaner, a tree ineptly planted at more than five degrees off a right angle to the earth.

Murderer. Tree hater, he yelled. You should replant.

I looked at his neck, the solid trunk of it, the sinew of muscle; it was a logger's neck. Joe and Ed had them too. I said, I don't cut them down, at least. You're the logger.

He shot me a mock sneer. You kill the babies instead, he said. Are you going to pay for that cottage with this killing of baby trees?

Absolutely. I'm gonna pay for it however I have to.

Not so nice, he said. Not so good for the trees. He pulled his tobacco out, rolled up a cigarette and stood there for a time drawing in clouds of smoke and looking down at my work. Then, he flicked the butt away and leaned over, grabbed the leader of the culprit spruce. He pressed his foot into the earth by the side of it, trying to urge the soil to hold the tree up. Joe and Ed flitted by in their duct-taped Y-fronts, skin shining with greasy insect repellent and the baby oil they slathered on each other to trap unsuspecting blackflies.

H'lo there, they said in unison.

Why don't they wear any clothes? Willem glared at them.

They want attention, I explain. Isn't that right, boys? You crave attention?

No, Alma. Joe tucked his hand into his underwear waistband, sang, Oo-Oo-Oo.

Actually, we wanted to get a tan. Ed was pulling his underwear down in the back to show his tan line.

Just one between you? I asked.

Very funny, Alma.

Ha ha.

Alma?

Oh, Alma? Don't you think we're well-endowed?

They opened their arms and stood to face me, buttocks pushed forward to accentuate bulges barely concealed beneath the thin polycotton underwear made in some inconsequential country where small people heaved around massive bolts of gleaming white fabric and snipped and sewed the long day for a pittance so that these two morons could prance about in it, shoving their genitals more or less in my face to get a reaction. So unfair. I stared. I stared and stared and stared.

Alma?

I'm not done, I said. I stared on, a grin breaking victoriously along my lips. I was curious to see if they'd get embarrassed and turn away, become fed up with the loss of time, time during which they could be earning a decent wage, or whether the attention would affect their manhood, whether a pair of simultaneously erecting members would entertain its audience. I was not disappointed. Joe and Ed rose as one. Willem turned away and started digging about in the dirt. I clapped my hands together.

Wonderful! Wonderful performance!

Thank you.

Thank you.

They bowed, as best they could under the circumstances, then smirked a bit and curtseyed. Off they went. I could hear Osho's voice on the wind, fuck you, fuck you, as Joe and Ed started a low rendition of a Pink Floyd song they had been practising all week; they had managed to sing it as a round — a really astonishing accomplishment. They were moving away into the distance, their erections, I supposed, slowly dying in their underpants as the song rose in volume toward its inevitable climax, Osho's fuck-you a static metronome pulsing in the background.

I am embarrassed of man, Willem muttered, shaking his head. It is terrible to be a man. He squatted, huddled around a little sapling, placing handfuls of black soil in clumps around its base, soil he had gathered from under a severed root.

Ach, it's just a joke, I said.

Not funny, he said.

I didn't mean it badly. Besides, they don't mind. They like it.

That is even more worse. Willem patted the black soil around the miniature tree trunk.

I'm sorry, I said. And I did feel sorry for my behaviour now that it was too late to do anything about it.

No sorry, he said, looking up at me. It isn't your fault.

I said, It isn't theirs either. They can't help it.

You must hate them to treat them like this.

No, I love men. I do, I love them to pieces.

Ortwin came wandering though the corridors, climbing over the slash heaps using his shovel as a walking stick, pushing burdock aside with it. He was checking quality, trying to maintain a level of camaraderie with the crew. He had sensed creeping demoralization in the air. The bear had snubbed the delicate reek of dead meat in the cage for the warm scent of the cook's tent. It'd been witnessed waddling away from the cook-shack on its hind legs, like some live animation, clutching a garbage can in its paws. We were advised to keep in groups or pairs at all times on the campsite; the forester came by and read a couple of bear mauling anecdotes to us. Ortwin had his own story about bears — a hungry west coast grizzly that had treed him and a tree runner. The brown bear had sat at the foot of the tree waiting for them to fall like ripened cherries. The tree runner never lived to tell the tale. These anecdotes were gruesome reminders of the food chain and where exactly we fit in. Ortwin dug up a couple of trees to check the roots. He walked the spacing. He tested the tightness of a few trees; everything was okay.

What's up with the bear? I said.

They're going to shoot him.

I thought about how the bear would look as it lay dying and dead, thought back a few summers when I had watched some hunters up from Pennsylvania moving in slow dance-like patterns around a bear carcass they had strung by the hind legs in a tree outside their lodge. They had cut the animal down the belly and removed its entrails.

That was a male, one of the hunters said, his accent memorable for its whiny shrillness and its nasal pronunciation.

I'm keeping his dingle as a trophy, he added, smiling, holding up the small glistening pink shaft. He was a happy infant with a new, as yet unexplored toy.

You're going to stuff it?

I ain't gonna stuff it. Can't. I'll just let it shrivel up. Atrophy, if you'll excuse the pun, little lady.

His buddies laughed and raised their beer bottles in salute to the bear.

Fine bear, they said.

Goddamn fine animal, they said, shaking their heads and tilting back their beer.

Defence strategies against angry bears included making yourself large by jumping around maniacally and yelling; bears have bad eyesight and are generally timid. After you had made yourself enormous, screamed like a banshee, thrown whatever large, hard object you may have at hand, then you were meant to play dead. This inevitably confused the bear into thinking you were dead. This last bit worried me. First of all, bears were known to store away fresh dead things for future use. Like humans, they preferred the taste of slightly fermented flesh. They'd be doubly pleased by a sudden, if inexplicable, demise. Second, why would a bear be convinced of your death if you had, just moments before, been tossing clumps of earth and sticks in her direction? Third, it made you an easy target. But for all that, I would follow the strategy, not because I thought it sane, but because I knew in situations of intense fear, my natural instinct was to acquiesce, to freeze. Black bears almost never attacked humans. This was a comfort.

Why kill the bear? I said to Ortwin. He only wants to eat.

He's already habituated to our camp garbage. He will get braver. Yeah, I said. Like a bear goes into a bar joke. He comes into the dining tent and sits down at one of the tables, and using human utensils, he eats, politely and without spilling, an entire human meal in the correct order, beginning with an aperitif and ending with a cognac and a moderate portion of fine dark chocolate. Afterwards, if the mood strikes, he will cut the snub end off a Havana cigar and smoke the entire stogie down without inhaling, before retiring to bed. My Fair Bear.

Ortwin laughed. He had taken a bundle of my trees and was firing them into the ground. With no apparent struggle, showing a delicate respect for the tools and the job, he moved silently, shovel-screefing the turf and duff away and slipping the trees into the ground. His arms were bare and brown, the muscles undulating naturally beneath the skin; his eyes were glinting with amusement and focus as twenty-five trees slid into new homes. In fifty years, these saplings would be a crop to be harvested, tree on tree in perfect array, soldiers waiting to be hewn down for the greater good of what? See, though, the arms, the rippling muscles. I kept my attention there, even as I felt the miserable, futile beauty of the scene overwhelm me.

Who will kill the bear?

The only guy'll do it's an Indian from way over in Powassan. Otherwise the season didn't start yet, no permits. Indian's gotta be able to see the bear's eyes before he'll shoot.

Willem said, *We* should move our camp.

It wouldn't make any difference, Ortwin said. Then he said something in Dutch to Willem that made Willem click his tongue in disapproval. That moment, Paul burst through a scraggy patch of undergrowth, his face shining with dirt, insect repellent and sweat, the look of a psychotic in his eyes.

I can't see my tape, he whispered. Where is it? I'm lost, lost.

Calm down, Paul. I'll get you back on track. Ortwin held him by the shoulder. I wanted to cry from looking at his forearm, the ripple of motion along it.

Calm down? Paul said. Calm down? His ruddy beard stubble stuck out like a half-inch lawn perpendicular to the topography of his face. He was mud-splattered, his pupils so dilated it was impossible to distinguish the colour of his eyes.

We waited for him that night, not so patiently, in the crummies. The windows were slightly open. Karl drew his thumb over single, unlucky blackflies as they tossed themselves on the windows, trying to get out, smearing them into small streaks of who knows whose blood. It was Clara who found Paul and pulled him out of the muck. His corpulent body had fallen through a sinking pool of swamp mud, and the struggle to get free had mired him up to the waist in cold earth. He had spent hours trying, to no avail, to grasp whatever weeds and small trees might provide some anchor, some leverage, but his dwindling weight was still too much to be pulled out that way. He was frantic by the time she hauled him out.

For hours, I just stayed very still, he said. Tried to remain calm. It was Clara saved me, really. I'd a been a goner, I s'pose. I've got Clara to thank.

He drank down the dregs of everyone's canteens, said he was dead thirsty, hadn't had a spot to drink, no water at all, and in that hot sun. The mud had already dried in blotches here and there on his trousers; the wet pants clung to his chubby legs. He glanced affectionately at Clara, patted her discreetly on the head as one might a small child.

Don't mention it, she said, with a certain pride. She straightened her workshirt, fiddled with the buttons, undoing the top one and then, apparently on second thought, doing it up again. She looked up to see me watching her and flushed pink. Paul was watching too.

Felt like bloody Tantalus, he said. Up to me arse in muck, not a drop in sight.

Stanley came up from Powassen and waited in camp for the animal to show. The bear complied in this way only, for in all other ways he refused to cooperate in his own death. He wouldn't turn to face his maker. Several times Stanley had the rifle cocked and ready, sights lined up, but the bear shifted his face away and turned, waggling his ass, some wicked bear joke. Once he curled his behind, arched his back and, wild berries and human food mixed in a messy cascade, evacuated his entire colon. Stanley lowered his sights.

Goddamn smart bear, he said. I don't like to kill him. He won't face me. I doubt if it's going to work out for us, me and him.

The weather was baking hot. Out in the field, the plots ranged from swamp to dry clay beds, the soil either so wet you got a soaker before you began the day, or so dry the dust puffed up and choked you. The earth, as you opened it, cracked like an unfired clay pot. How anything was supposed to grow in this was beyond the understanding of mortal man, but the foresters were experts, eh? The foresters and the pulp mill owners who were obliged to replant the harvested tracts.

Keep planting. It's on the map we got, they said.

I just did what I was told, cog in the wheel. Willem moaned about it — not the work, the drudgery, the pain of the weather, the bugs and the blisters that had formed even on his logger's calluses but the simple plight of little trees as they dried up and died behind us.

This is so stupid, he said.

We kept finding Clara and Paul together in our corridors, lost. They had joined ranks, Paul because he felt indebted and figured he couldn't beat it, so why not join it, and Clara because she liked to feel needed and be indebted to and because she liked the feeling of feeling sorry for someone. Love? She'd taken to wearing her day-off shirt — a crisp, pale purple cotton blouse with ruffles down the front. She was out of place and marvellous as she flounced about putting trees in randomly wherever she sensed they were needed.

Hi guys, how are you doing? she said as she planted up to us.

Paul sighed, We're in your corridor, then, aren't we? Come on, Clara. And as they turned around and walked back to try to find their own area, he muttered, Hey, Alma. How many trees so far? And when I answered, he said, I can't bloody believe it. You must be stashing.

There were many forms of stashing. There was the unavoidable angst-stash in which the planter, out of sheer frustration at the endless horror of the job, hurled a tree or two into a thicket by way of relief. There was the stash in which the planter calculatingly opened a gash in the closest quagmire, usually by the roadside where the earth was pretty churned up by all-terrain vehicles bringing trees into the site, and jabbed several bundles into this opening. This sealed straightaway, earthly lips shutting forever. There was the stash in which the crew boss quietly beckoned a planter or two to stay in camp for a per diem bribe and set them the task of physically macerating bagloads of saplings, had them stuff the debris into green garbage bags, load these onto a crew truck and toss them into a pit at the local dump. There was the subtle unspoken stash in which the boss left the planter in an isolated landscape with a certain number of trees, too many for the site, gave the planter a knowing wink and said, in passing, that he wasn't planning on bringing any trees back out. There was the stash in which at the end of a contract an uncalculated number of leftover trees had become slimy with fungus. These were unceremoniously dumped in a backwoods hole. The waste factor at work. Of course it was all illegal. Of course everyone was guilty — guilty at least with the peripheral knowledge that this was done.

Stashing? I said. What do you know about stashing?

Poor little trees. Paul looked forlorn. I noticed the hair on his face had lost its natural lustre. It looked dead.

One way or another, I said, it's seven cents, isn't it?

I like to think of it as a quarter-ounce bend, he said.

You do look fine, Paul. Wait until your wife sees you.

She's filing for divorce, actually. No worries. I'll manage.

He looked over at Clara and smiled. She smiled in return. So much for secrets.

Ah, well.

I set the mass of dry nettle stalk to ret and within days the rotting enzyme began its work. I laid it in a semicircle on the grass outside my tent to dry. That went pretty fast, the weather was so bloody hot. I had my scutched, carded product in no time and began to spin again, this time long, increasingly perfect coils of thread. It had nubble and snubs of bark and would never be considered a fine yarn, but I didn't care. I was that close to success.

Chapter Fourteen

June 10. She was always pretty kind even when I wasn't. I admit I was a toad, no amount of kissing will help me. I'm not a prince, though I ought by all rights to be one — that's another story best left out of this. You wouldn't believe it anyhow. Delusion is the old-fashioned term for it. I call it truth but that's the way I look at it. How you look at a thing is everything, isn't it? Perspective.

Her breasts! I fantasize about them. She's nice to the old man, how she shares the little cherub. He looks like me around the eyes. I've named him Hendrik. After Opa. In this way I will bring back the dead. When she ran off at the end of the contract, oh, they sent teams of people in to look for her. Had she gone mad like the pioneers, like the moose racing out of the bug-infested forest? I knew. I could hear her calling me. And when I came back up this year, I couldn't stand it, the voices were so persistent. The sound travelled just between my skin and God. You believe in God, don't you? There is a pattern to everything, yes? It can't be avoided.

Along with the newspaper, Jake has brought back vodka and mix, and we've been cutting out for two days and nursing headaches for four, a blur of joviality and retching. The fact is, I cannot really tolerate drink. I try to pace myself. I believe my breast milk is intoxicating too, for Adam has been listless and, thankfully, quiet. We are on a hiatus of drink, planet drink. We are deep into it the first night and Jake is describing his youth.

With one hand he gestures, with the other he changes a diaper. The wolves are howling and the bugs are throwing themselves at the window, desperate for the light.

I could have married any one of them, Jake says. My skin was smoother than Mosie's here. Mosie's baby butt. Now I'm old. Underneath the wrinkles and the calluses and the dry leather skin, there's a young man there.

Has he infiltrated my mind? There he is again, transforming underwater into a golden Adonis. Jake, the great traveller. Jake, the illusionist. Jake, the figment of my imagination.

Adam, I say. His name is Adam. I'm sure I'm slurring, the drink is pulsing at my skin.

Moses. To me his name is Moses.

It's my kid.

Progress, he says, nodding.

He holds up the cloth he is using to wipe the boy and a waft of shit passes by me. For what it's worth, he says, and tosses the cloth and the diaper into a bucket we have set just inside the front door. For what it's worth, I believe she died happy. She was on the verge of heaven and then there it was unfolding before her. For her.

I do not immediately catch on to the fact he is talking about the fat lady on the *Titanic*, whose death he is ultimately responsible for. And then, in my drunken thoughts, I see Jake take her in his young arms and slide his hand up under her dress, beneath the elastic apparatus that holds her stocking up. She tosses her head back in anticipation of the contact he will make, his fingertips on her sex. Her body is arched toward him.

Is heaven ecstatic? I say. This is having an effect on me.

I think it must be.

That strikes me as a cop-out. I say this to keep the rush of moisture at bay.

What?

You're making your fantasy work for you, to absolve you of your own immorality.

She was having a good time . . .

Still. I mean how good a time could she have been having? She's dead, after all.

I have achieved it. I have found the button to his brutality. The clitoris of his brutality! He spits a mouthful of vodka onto the floor at my feet. He heaves the door open and he is gone into the night. I hear him stumble and swear and then I hear nothing. He has dissipated into the night. I'm thrilled until I discover that the door is ripped off the shack and that I am now vulnerable to everything. I hear the night creatures encroaching, either in fact or not, hear them moving toward the house, sense their nostrils pondering the smell of my skin. I strap the baby to my waist and rock back and forth to the rhythm of the coursing of booze through my system. I'm libidinous and drunk and terrified, and the creatures are encroaching.

Oh Adam, Adam, I moan. I am moaning. The depths of degradation to which I have succumbed. I am aware that the baby is all I have and even he is not mine. Later, much later, the boy watching me with wide open eyes, I hear a thrashing in the woods. I am paralyzed. But it is only Jake; soon he begins to shout obscenities at the moon. Or at me. That's possible. My drunkenness has digressed to something less, the boundaries of my body have evaporated, and I am only fear and adrenaline and sex. Exponential night terror, and still the boy's eyes stare like an insistent doll up at my face. He seems asleep, wide asleep.

She was my martyr, he yells. She died so I could live. I've done that for her, haven't I? Not for one second did I allow myself to die. I never let down. I honoured our pact. Didn't I?

You killed her, I scream.

She wasn't alive, I tell you. She'd been as good as dead long before we ever met.

I don't hear him anymore. Well, I hear him mumbling, but not what he's saying, and after listening into the night for a while, I begin to melt into the sounds I hear until I am asleep. I know this because I eventually wake up and it is day. My first thought is of my mother suffocating into her chesterfield. Push this away. A thin artery of pain connects the front of my cranium with the back. I am good for nothing and lie on my bed with Adam, feeding him and sleeping in turn. Later, when I get up, I half rejoice. I have made Jake angry! I know that this is a great and practical achievement, though I do not yet know to what end I have achieved it. He himself slinks home in mid-afternoon with a skinned rodent — a chipmunk? — hanging from a stick and a grin breaking out over his face. I am weaving and pretend not to look up. It is an axe I've woven, Guilbert's axe, made diagonally corner to corner; it looks like a ghost axe, an axe a ghost would wield.

> ⚹ When Guilbert heard about the countess stopping the shroud's progress he was at wits' end. He believed the countess no more capable of altering the Wolf's nasty momentum than of turning the ocean's tide. Quietly, stealthily, he went hunting.

Jake is boiling the meat in a pot on the stove. He hovers over it, sprinkling herbs from the garden. Thyme by the smell of it. He will throw lamb's quarters and plantain in as well for iron and roughage. He is big into roughage. The soup smells wretched, bilious, or is that me? He turns. I can feel him staring at the back of my head. In fact my hackles are up, little neck hairs standing straight out.

There was a great bear with me last night.

Jake, you were drunk.

And blind? he says. Don't forget who catches dinner.

But not bear, surely. That's a small bear. I indicate the soup. It's missing something, too, some tang, I say. We are silent for a time, and I continue to work.

    On her cloth, Renelde did not include the scene in which Guilbert returned to the castle, his axe tucked into his breeches — the scene in which he made his brazen attempt at murder. Guilbert's behaviour was too foolish for her to examine. The cook's apprentice relayed the story to the mill boy who whispered it to the baker and on through the land until it reached Renelde as some distant episode that may or mayn't have had anything to do with her at all. The cry that went up from Burchard. Like a wailing child, or worse, a woman. Guilbert rose up out of nowhere, he had crept so silently, had left his clogs at Renelde's hut and gone barefoot. The wound he inflicted was glancing and ineffectual, a simple flesh injury that did not kill the Wolf but instead sufficed to banish the woodcutter for as long as the Wolf lived to repay the favour. Guilbert fled, stinking of lavender and lanolin. Renelde had daubed him later that same night with oil of lavender and rubbed him with unwashed wool, a sensual disguise designed to keep Burchard's hounds at bay, the hounds they could already hear barking outside Locquinol, in the Mormal forest. Guilbert the woodcutter was not seen in those parts for two years.

I recall some important story — the story about the bear at the treeplanting camp — and I tell it to Jake. But as I finish and we begin to eat our chipmunk broth, which tastes as scuttling as the beast itself, I think no. I think I know why I am so pleased to have made Jake angry.

They have returned, I say.

He knows who I'm talking about. He looks at me and picks Adam up off the end of the table where he lies sleeping and hands him to me.

You should go home to your mother.

A jibe about my mother. Interesting. He has my ticket but not the power to activate it. I'm too far.

They are walking in the wasteland not far south from here, I say. They are filling in the spaces and soon, Jake, there won't be anywhere for you, either. It will all be forest. Filled. No spaces in between for you.

The bear spoke to me, he says.

Oh?

He said that he loved you, said the boy was rightfully his, implored me to hand him over.

Oh?

Yes. Called him Hendrik. Who is he?

No, Jake, listen. The land will get so filled with trees and undergrowth, you will be forced to appear. You will be found, you will not be able to hide any longer. I rap my hand on the table for emphasis.

Who is he? he yells.

None of your business.

Oh, it is.

Jake is gone the next day, but that doesn't stop me from shouting at him, for I know he is there, somewhere in the bush, listening. Perhaps he's gone back to read the mine shaft book, to find out from it what he's been doing from a different point of view. That it isn't there anymore will perplex him; I see him frantically feeling around with his little paws, going deeper and deeper into the pit for nothing.

I shout, He's mine, you fucker.

I hear a replying rustle and scan the edge of the forest. Am I still drunk? Am I bushed? No. It's him. Tunnel dweller, book scribbler. The waft of garlic never exorcised such a one. Garlic. It is in the air. Adam's face is turned toward it, his arms have lifted to reach toward it.

No! I gather him up even as he coos and I run with this bundle back to the shack.

It's a bear, a bear, a bear. I whisper it to him by way of convincing myself.

Jake! Stop hiding, I yell. The bear has come back. Adam . . . Moses is frightened!

Suddenly I smell garlic over everything. Is it the soup? It occurs to me suddenly what it's missing.

Nettle, I yell. Jake does not respond.

Nettle!

I gather Adam up and trundle off to the forest periphery, act like I'm not looking for Jake, act like I couldn't care less, stoop here and there where I see fresh nettle. I know how to pick it so it doesn't burn. It burns anyhow.

I'm making the best soup, I yell.

No Jake. The nettle, thrown in at the last minute, gives the broth a sharp spinach flavour. Come on, Jake, I mumble as I eat. Come back. I eat alone. There is a faint odour on the breeze that is not soup, is maybe just warm air, earth and watching eyes. It is the smell of tangibility.

July 8. See her stoop and bend, see her swim, it's like a painting. Sweet nostalgia. Sweet sepia wet dream. The mine shaft was soaking up my seed for thinking of her. How long must I wait? That day in the crummy when we waited for that fat Australian circus performer. He had dugs. I'd seen him in the shower. It's revolting how self-indulgent some people are, really. I don't like to tell this.

It happened then. I noticed her arm pressed up against Willem's arm and I sensed it. There was electricity. I couldn't handle this and started to run my fingers over blackflies and draw their little carcasses out over the windows. It was that or cry. I was a participant before that, don't you see? Then suddenly I was relegated to being the voyeur. I was watching myself fall apart. But I knew somehow he was temporary, that he had no true dignity, that like a flower to the sun, her face would turn back toward me.

Chapter Fifteen

Osho stayed home, ostensibly with a treeplanter's wrist cramp, but in fact he spent the day lying in wait for the creature and eventually shot it with the camp rifle that was kept for emergencies in the office tent. This created a brief upset for a variety of reasons, not the least of which was that Osho had neither a hunting nor a gun licence. In what appeared to be a premeditated act, he had broken the lock to the gun case with a stone and lain quietly in wait to destroy the bear. Marilene witnessed the violence from the door of the cookshack and began to wail. The bear was a bristle of twitching fur, shuddering in its death throes. Osho rocked back and forth laughing like a madman, his tie-dyed orange button-down shirt flapping in the summer breeze. The bear was dead.

Marilene shouted, How could you do that? You're a vegetarian.

I thought you loved me, he yelled back.

That's beside the point, she said. I thought you loved animals. I thought we agreed here. Marilene's apron was wet with the insipid pink of chicken blood. It was fajita night.

I love animals, he screeched. I love you. He was crying, the way men cry when they don't want to, his face a contortion of holding.

Osho sat staring at the bear corpse until the crews drove in. Ortwin talked him into giving up the gun. It was rumoured that he intended to commit suicide with it if Marilene didn't come around, but in fact the rifle was a single shot. The barrel was empty and he didn't have any ammunition anyway, didn't even know how to load the thing. Stanley came in from Powassen and told the ministry forester that he killed the bear. The moment of death was fudged. Stanley winched the carcass up into the back of his rusty red pickup.

My wife is going to be pretty happy for the freezer meat, Stanley said. There was a thin trail of dark blood on the ground behind the truck. The animal looked as if it was sleeping, its paws pointing skyward in a strange wave as the truck pulled out and receded down the bumpy dirt road.

The death did not stem the rising tide of anxiety in the camp. I had attributed this growing tension to the bear's unpredictable presence, but I was mistaken. A verbal jostling of which I had previously been unaware rose to a pitch that was unavoidable — bitter, rancorous comments were whispered between planters, and although the context of these gossips was petty and inconsequential, they created an unsettled environment. The weather too was unbearable. We ran out of drinking water before the heat of the afternoon reached its apex. It was not uncommon to encounter sweaty, half-clad planters; Joe and Ed were no longer anomalous. Clara passed us with a furrowed brow and duct tape wrapping each breast into a cone; her skin glistened with baby oil, half-dead blackflies writhed on her.

Iron woman, she said. I nodded. Paul planted up the rear, stooped in perfect, rhythmic timing to her stoop, a moronic smile cutting across his stubbled face. There was an increase in the time-honoured game of musical tents. It became impossible to predict where anyone might be at any given time. Nightly moans lifted into the still, dark night. I alone, I supposed, remained true to myself, pumping away at the ever-more-ethereal sexual fantasy of Ortwin's arms, the owner of which had himself found dubious solace in the arms of a local tree runner who wore a wide-brimmed leather hat and whistled "Motorcycle Mama." Ortwin had hired him from the Hearst Nightclub. And sweet

Jesus. He fit right into the mix. Karl, my nemesis, was the only other celibate besides Osho, who was in the doghouse for killing the bear, and Willem, who, it turned out, had a girl back home.

She's not exactly a girlfriend, he said.

Karl reached out to me in the crummy and ran his finger along the side of my neck.

I don't know about you, my friend, he said, but I'm so horny I could fuck a moose.

As I lay in my tent that night, a moose did come right up and rustle the nylon of my dome house with its muzzle. I hissed and it bounded off into the bush. I caught a glimpse of its long elegant legs picking through the understory, my face framed in the zippered archway of the tent door. It made me think of Osho, his long legs clad in ochre jogging pants, his angst dance though the day, spear-chucking, cursing the gods, and of how this one act of disobedience, this bear shooting had somehow created him in my mind. I saw him clearly now, sitting in lotus position, the rifle resting on his shoulder, a beatific grin forming. How suddenly he came into being.

Willem no longer needed my workaday advice, but we had grown used to one another and tended to plant together. I still put my trees in twice as quickly as he did, and so we were separated for long periods of time. While I filled in the back of our corridors, he moved at right angles to my activity. In this way I moved in and out of his orbit through the day, sometimes so deep in thought, thoughts I would be hard-pressed to describe if asked, so fleeting were they, that when I came upon him, I was often surprised. We exchanged little pleasantries or comments designed to keep informed about the lay of the land. I was used to these meetings and looked forward to them; one was utterly alone otherwise. It was good to hear the sound of another voice, rumbling and low, in contrast to the shrill, sad call of the white-throated sparrow, the hush of breeze, the clack of grasshopper or the rising croak of a frog and then frogs as the mating symphony rose and then died down. Even the frogs, yes.

Ortwin drove us deep into the contract site, back to the last several hectares, and left us with enough trays of container stock to plant double the area, an obvious ploy to get rid of overstock. He drove off, the ATV spluttering and whining, scaring off wildlife — the large but not the small variety. The bugs felt the noise as an intense vibration, which seemed to excite them even more. The heat had burned off most of the blackflies and mosquitoes; we contended with horseflies, deerflies and no-see-ums, which swarmed or dive-bombed as per their own instinct. I no longer felt their penetrations; I was inured. But Willem swiped hopelessly at them while loudly bawling them out in Flemish.

The first thing I did when the last of the ATV dust settled and Ortwin was out of sight was hoist a tray of tree plugs onto my back and lumber into the forest with them. The undergrowth was green and thick and the trees I scattered there were un-detectable. I made sure Willem saw this. I forced him to count some of these trees on his day tally; it would look suspicious to have such a huge sum on my plate.

I don't know why you are doing this, Alma.

You want to cart all these out at the end of the day?

We could at least plant them in the forest.

And if the MNR sees you foraging about in the forest plant-ing trees? Forget that. It's not pragmatic.

It goes against the nature, he said.

Nature? I asked. What is nature? There is no nature anymore.

It was a beautiful day. The ground all around us was mercifully soft and fertile. We were in paradise, creamland. All we had to do was scrape the tiniest layer of grass from the earth to find topsoil of the finest quality. The trees went in like magic and I was tranced out. The little wrapped-up container-stock roots were easily poked in. Creamland! Race, race, my body removed itself and I was pure thought floating above the work. I hurtled forward, my body adrenal with the excitement of motion through space. It was as if I was planting all my trees simultaneously, they went in that fast. The gapes of earth sent luscious puffs of soil smells up into my nostrils as I shut them with my toe. I ran, sweat coming up in beads and rolling down my face. I did not bother to wipe this sweat away. I let it run in rivulets, felt it trickle down from my armpits and wick into my filth-encrusted cotton undershirt.

We took the outer edges of the field, and every so often I stood up, pulled my hair away from my face and scanned the territory for Willem. He was stooping or rising, our perspective on one another growing as the morning wore on. It was getting towards the end of the contract. I felt inclined to hurry, make that last pile of coin, increase my unemployment premium. The rush. Money. Tree. Money. Tree. I bent forward to the next microsite; there was no big picture. Willem and I sat together at lunch, sat on our treeplanting bags, wet soil drying on our fingers as we ate, drying under our nails. I peeled back the duct tape and examine the dimpled, pink skin of my fingers, like a child's after a long bath. Willem had his shirt off. I noticed tiny, almost imperceptible extra nipples, six in all, lined up like an animal's down his stomach, and, gesturing with my own strange skin, I mentioned this to him.

He drew his pinky from one to the next, connecting them like a dot-to-dot.

I was meant to be born to a dog, he said. An animal without thought or worry.

We didn't talk much. The sun made us sleepy, and besides, we were tired. The night before there had been a party of sorts in the cookshack, and both of us had taken the opportunity to drink a few glasses of crappy wine, not enough to get drunk but enough to sap energy from the next day's work. There was dancing. Clara turned up the volume on a blaster, some tune from the seventies with a deep pelvic rhythm, and suddenly everyone found themselves dancing.

"I Believe in Miracles."

Karl poked his hands, slightly offbeat, toward the plastic roof and swung his middle-aged butt back and forth, bumping people on purpose. Osho watched from a corner as Marilene shook herself and laughed. He rose and moved toward her and began to dance, head and hair flying, eyes shut, conjuring some personal conglomeration of gods. He moved closer and closer to her and she did not avoid him. I slept fitfully, the heat making my tent into a dry sauna and the evening not cooling down enough to make much of a difference. I ripped the tarp off the tent roof, but already too much heat had been trapped. I tossed and turned.

I could hear Osho and his friends in the valley beyond my tent, chanting. Someone had bells and was jangling them. I dreamt of oxen and a hay wagon that became something else, a man and then a bear. Osho and Marilene were celebrating. It was interfering with my sleep, their bacchanal, their loud sexual reconciliation. It frustrated me no end. The heat, the moans of the others, the very life urging up around me in the bush irritated me. Waking up, I smelled the alcohol oozing up with my sweat.

Willem and I were now edged by a forest of silver birch trees, the leaves of which shuddered, the sun reflected off them. I had already planted one thousand trees, not including what I tossed, sacrificed to the forest, and I felt justified in taking my time eating my lunch. I opened an Oreo cookie and, with my teeth, pulled the vanilla icing from the wafer. I sucked on this, relishing the sweetness on my tongue as the wad of icing melted and finally slid down my throat. The sun was warm.

I am leaving soon, Willem said suddenly. I won't be coming back, not soon, maybe never. Come with me. That cottage of your dreams. I will build it.

What? What about your girlfriend?

She's not my girlfriend. She was my girlfriend but now she's not.

Why are you leaving? I said. I had grown used to his lumbering form near me in the field, grown familiar with his body as it moved about around me. I had grown fond of him despite myself.

The ministry. They discovered I am working under false identity. It is to protect Ortwin. I am going home. Come. Come away with me. I really am liking you a lot.

I began to frown. And it was then that Willem moved his hand — the fingers of which were once, long ago, mangled by a chainsaw — moved it from his upper thigh, to my ear. And what began there ended in our lovemaking. I cannot say this was a complete surprise to me. I had been expecting something of the sort for some time. I had been waiting, creating, however inadvertently, the opportunity for this. It is impossible to describe the act of love and do it justice. It is either above or below vocabulary, freshly shocking that the union of two people is profound. What purpose would it serve to say his pinky gently followed the S-curve of my outer ear, working as a switch in turning on a circuit, and that my body flooded in anticipation? None. He tugged at the lobe and then went in behind the ear and, barely touching me, drew down the curve again and again, softly. His face was very close to mine and his eyes looked into my eyes for some sign that what he was doing was allowable, but with a slight worry evident in them, too, that even if it wasn't, he might not be able to stop himself. His hair had grown since I first saw him. It hung around his face in matted, uncombed tufts, the ends brushing along my lips.

Your ears are very pretty, he said. You know, I can't really stand this anymore.

I laughed, a short, surprised laugh that was more an exhalation than anything. He sat up and looked around, making sure we were alone and not likely to be disturbed. His hand ran up under my shirt and he pulled the cloth back.

Is it okay? he said. And then, Your nipples have little points. His hand was flat open on my belly, moving up and down with my breath.

I pulled him down by grabbing onto his hair. Our mouths meet in a slurry of wet, the cookie sweet between us, our tongues running along each other's teeth, soft on hard, a precursor to what followed. His penis arched up, the glans poking up out of its skin. See? What can one say that will not taint the experience? Could one say darling metaphorical things: we consumed one another? Or bawdy things: hung like a stallion, twice as eager? We gathered each other in. I held his waist like so. He put his palm there. His thumb there. He groaned when he felt the wetness. I shimmied my clothes off; he watched as if amazed, as if he had never seen this performed before, this same dance, the ritual of surprise, of renewed anticipation, seen it a hundred times before with other women, on television, in the movies, in books or naughty magazines found in the attic. His skin was like my own, reminding me of me, and we urged each other on within the slow and fast pulse of our desire in the ancient game of empty and full. Willem stopped himself short. He was wild-eyed.

He said, Can I stay?

In Canada?

No, in you.

How can I describe it in a way that doesn't diminish it? It was nothing. It was everything.

Ortwin seemed to sense our altered states when we returned to the crummy. He laughed in a particularly knowing way, huge and loud, and patted Willem on the back, his reason for doing so ambiguous. Sexual secrets were very hard to keep in a closed community. I felt Willem's sperm sliding out of my vagina as the van bumped down the pitted clay logging road. I smelled ocean salt too as it mingled with the other smells in the crummy: the reek of people coming out of the woods, of soil drying, of dry urine and shit and pesticide and bug-dope, sweat, spit and soap — the stench of nature mixed with the smell of change. There was Karl's breath too, his oppressive stare — the large yellow eyes of betrayal staring at the back of my head all the way home.

For one week, the point was not tree upon tree upon tree. It was open sky and fractured English and giddy happiness. Planting slowed to a near halt. Willem and I looked up from the bowers we created whenever the mood struck, we looked up from the little duff beds and wondered at the gorgeous low cumulus, the fragile blue sky and how it bore down on us. We stared out post-coital from the jutting debris of the slash heap that had just provided a wall, the necessary resistance to our rough acquiescence. We caught our breath and pointed up at a swirl of bird's wings on the wind stream and we were content.

When do you leave?

I don't want to talk.

No.

I wondered, even then, if our affection was buoyed by the reality of his departure. But when I suggested I come visit, he was not coy. We made plans together; we spoke of infinite futures. We looked forward. That week, time sped up. It was inevitable that it should as, in a way, it was timeless, a pocket in time, a subversion of all the banality one experiences when one is truly in the moment. If I may be permitted glibness, this was a fairy tale. This was outside of everything. We laughed when I recollected how ridiculous he seemed when I met him, but the fact was that he had not changed. I had. I had opened to him. And this opening was one I would quickly come to regret. Peer into any opening and see the abyss. A dark hole, a tunnel into the earth, shadowlands.

You will have your little house in Flanders, white paint and *kantwerk* curtains. The children will gather.

Papa, they will shout. Where is Papa?

I'll come home smelling of forest and . . .

. . . and mansweat.

. . . and they will ask me about the creatures. And I will tell them about the little moles and the hedgehogs and when they are old enough they will come and work with me and . . .

. . . the house will have a woodstove that leaks a bit of smoke and we will always smell of ash and . . .

. . . yes.

Ortwin lent the camp ATV to Willem and off we went. It was a thrill to move so quickly through the dense air, against the insectarium, against the heaviness of one's own body, a thrill to press myself in behind him and hold him, gain purchase on his body, tighter than necessary. We sped, the vehicle whipping us up whenever we hit roots and potholes in the old road. And then the clearing, the mine shaft pool. Even the inside of a weather-worn, decrepit, unhygienic hut can seem beautiful if one is in the right mood.

July 17. She was wearing a light blue man's shirt, a well-tailored business shirt with the old collar taken off. I remember her very well as she climbed up into the van, her leather steel-toed boot, scarred and open at the laces, stepping up into the van, and there was an alteration in her. A lightness. The fairies had taken her, my grandmother would have said. She was gone.

Chapter Sixteen

Adam is happy. I've never really noticed before that a baby can indicate happiness. Sleep is not happiness, as I had previously thought. Sleep is merely rest, recuperation, a place away for the purpose of reconvening one's sanity. It makes sense that Adam should need sleep. But why should he be happy? Has my plan entered him? Has he guessed what is afoot? I believe he is aware of everything. He is an appendage of me, a facet of me. It shocks me that he smiles.

I am weaving rather too quickly lately with some internal deadline I cannot really discuss. The cloth lies in squares of varying technical achievement. Paradoxically, some of the ones I more or less tossed off are most successful, while the bits I laboured over and fussed at are failures. It is too late to undo what I have done. The errors must speak for themselves. Below me as I work, Adam waves his fat arms and legs, reaching up toward the loom. The cloth grows in importance and I am focused there, but I can still hear his coos. I can smell his rank diaper, too. I will hold him over the sink and pump up water to clean him when I am done. For now I enjoy his little bird noises. Does a baby need both parents? Does it only feel whole when both halves are present? Push this thought away.

Burchard nursed his wound. Guilbert's axe had only grazed the cheek. Burchard counted himself lucky; if he'd shifted to the left the bastard would have split him down the centre like an oak sapling.

That's what you get, Guilbert had said.

Burchard trusted he wouldn't see him again.
The girl must have complained; it was nothing to
him. But it wouldn't make him gentler, for the
pain. There was an initial resonance of searing
pain down along his spine; he swore he thought
he'd died until the blood started. It took a linen
sheet to staunch it. A whole bloody sheet. That
damn rogue — he was fortunate to have his head.
The scar would render Burchard uglier than ever.
But that was nothing to him either. He would have
Renelde weave another sheet and then pay her
in kind for both the wound and the discomfort.

Yes!

Since Guilbert fled, Burchard's hounds at his
heels, baying, Burchard felt uncannily alive. Had
the brush with death bred immortality? The answer
was simple: the girl must have stopped her weaving.
Ahh, life! He felt so vigorous after his ill-ness that
he decided to take a ride in the fresh air. He went
to Renelde, all the way thinking, If only she'd come
to me. And was it only his imagination, or, when
he did confront her, was the certain timidity she
had previously displayed evaporating, did she act
as if she had some power over him, the little slut?

Renelde was standing at the back of the cottage,
beside the loom. He liked the way her hair fell in
subtle waves along her shoulders, curling under her
neck. He demanded to know where the woodcutter
had run, but she only pretended dismay, something
he was pleased to react to. He felt suddenly skin-hot
with the theatrics of it. Which made him suspicious
of her.

You aren't weaving again, are you?

No, sir . . .

She ran her finger along the dust that had
settled atop the material and showed it to him
as proof. Little specks fell to the floor, visible in a
diffuse beam of light entering the window.
Burchard had torn a swatch of bedding and was
holding it up to his cheek through the whole encounter, pulling it away now and again to show
her the wound. He had hoped she would gasp and
tend to him, but she only stared. He began to sway
and would have fallen down right there in the room
from the pain and loss of blood had he not called
out in time to his carriage driver for help.

I wish Jake would come back, though I'm thrilled to have pissed
him off so heartily. Adam's fallen asleep and I step out into the
day. The pile of wolf scat to the left of the door has sprouted
several long-stemmed mushrooms, the roots anchored atop single
dried droppings. Out of shit, life! I stand between the garden and
the shack, and for the first time in a great long time, I turn and
survey the structure. It looks like the cabin of a boat tilted in a
storm. The outer walls are buckled in mimicry of a tree, as if the
boards seek their tree time. It is a grievous thing, this structure,
the windows of which stare blankly out at me, at nothing.

It is warm, the sun warms me and I think of Willem. I
imagine him plundering the forests of Europe, a small creature-
like man under a vast canopy. I wonder if he misses me, if he ever
thinks of me. Do silent tears course his face with each crashing
tree? If there are eyes watching me, and I suspect there are, I have
reason to believe I am not crazy in this suspicion, if these eyes
were his I would languish in them. Oh, the sun is hot. I go to
the edge of the mine pool. There is an allure to the water and
I strip off my clothing, briefly running a hand over the post-
partum ribbing along my belly, over my lopsided breasts. I take

my time. I stand basking in the sun. No. I stand naked for his eyes, as I imagine them staring me in. And then I walk into the dead sea as if it is a beach until the eroding edge gives way and I am sucked down. The water is as skin to me.

July 19. It lasted about a week. It was heartbreaking. You have no idea. She came around though. I knew she would. I never gave up. I don't. I'm a tenacious optimist. The candle stub will go out any second, already it is flickering. Writing faster and faster. On the floors, the walls. Oh vision! Oh vision, the boy's arms climbing the air toward me. I remember her and that lumberjack in the woods, how she undressed, took off all her clothes and stood, a vision of pink, scratches and bruises, and those impossible tits that I'd . . .

She knew I was there. She must have. It took everything to stay still, not to frighten her away. Minutes going on forever, she stood there, nipples hard in the wind, I thought she might touch herself. I hoped she would let her hands linger along the curves of her body and . . .

I tried to make it happen with my mind, now. I got caught up in that. To pump or not to pump. I could hear my own little noises, the little grunts, I'm not proud of it. She never moved, fists at her sides. And then she seemed to fall. I imagine her falling into the water, devoured by the mine shaft pool. I reached out to save her . . .

Oh, it was beautiful.

Oh, it was beautiful.

Oh, it was beautiful.

Ahh. It gives me such heaven.

Chapter Seventeen

Ortwin came into the cookshack midway through dinner and requested twenty volunteers to fight a small forest fire in one of our blocks. When no one volunteered, he pulled out a list, read it and thanked us for our cooperation. We crammed water tanks, extra hoses, water barrels into one of the crummies and loaded ourselves, mildly excited, into the two other vehicles. There was talk of fire duty compensation, and the prospect of bonus earnings added an air of festivity to the occasion. Ortwin looked around at us.

I don't know how it started, he said, but it was likely a cigarette.

The rising telltale smoke was first spotted by Osho, who then stayed behind with Clara and Paul to try to contain it. This was a hopeless task. The smoke was already billowing when we got there, and Osho, Paul and Clara were shiny black — ash sticking to sweat. They'd run out of water and were now futilely scrambling to dig over the earth, in some places attempting to sever, with dull axes and shovel blades, entire tree roots of potential fuel.

I thought back over that day, the rich contentment of it, our last day as I came to think of it later, the satisfying, unthinking, lush, hot end to it, the laughing bemusement of our mutterings and the way Willem's cigarette looked as it arced and then, the friction of the air breaking its trajectory, plummeted to earth. I did not rise as I had before to press the back of my heel into the slow-burning butt. I believed, where I had never believed before, that it would consume itself and die, that it would not burn on, and that if it did, this event would be somehow separate from me, somehow none of my business, a fire out of control on a newscast inside the box of a distant television — nothing, nothing to do with me.

Osho said, Uh, Christ eh? Who's the bastard who didn't put his cigarette out right?

Willem looked up at me through the tangle, the unintentional dreadlock of hair that fell in braid-like mats over his cheeks. He was working madly, the aura of guilt palpable. He dug in furiously, as if single-handedly trying to put a stop to this danger that he had unwittingly unleashed. Osho had the look in his eye that killing the bear gave him, the look of a man without values, none.

You smoke? he said to Willem. Don't you?

Yes, I smoke. It was perhaps my cigarette that will cost us the evening sleeping. I can't say it for sure.

Was this your corridor?

I can't say for sure. But it was; we knew it was. Our bodies had pressed into the earth here. Perhaps there was still an imprint of evidence. The fire edged toward us under the dry duff, the dusty composting needles of years ago. It surfaced every now and again, licks of flame eating the very air. We could hardly breathe. The wind, not present during the day, all but still, somehow managed to twist the smoke and fling it in every direction so we could scarcely remain clear of it long enough to take in a clean breath. The fire where the wind pushed it, along with the smoke — this was the side that we were attempting to control, spurting futile little sprays of water that sizzled into the air and seemed only to enrage the thing. How fast could the worms dig down to safety?

Look, yelled Osho, gesturing wildly at the fire as it climbed slash, the whoosh of air sucked into itself. Look. Look. What you did.

Leave him alone, Osho. If he did it, it was an accident. I stood between them.

Osho threw his shovel into the ground then and shouted, railed, screamed. He was an idealist confronting another idealist on the issue of reality.

This was not what I expected, he rasped.

The fire was swiftly edging toward us, a low, moving wall of orange and blue heat. Our trenches were hopeless, couldn't be completed fast enough to make a bit of difference. The fire did not so much leap them as tunnel under them, finding fuel somewhere deep within the ground. Ortwin rigged a hose system up to a small swamp, and then we could at least pump water at a decent rate, try to keep the burn contained — a vessel of fire, which we hoped would exhaust its own resources and expire. I soaked a cotton rag I had torn away from my T-shirt and held it up to my face. I wheezed — the air that the fire voraciously consumed was replaced with curling smoke. Clean air had a particular sweet odour I had never before noticed. The gasping wall of smoke interfered with its pleasures. Each breath was a precious achievement, a have-not. Ortwin removed Osho, the fiery rage of him, to the swamp, where he spent his time manning the little generator that had been rigged to the pump. He had to keep moving the pump's hose as the small swamp thickened into mud.

In the middle of that night, while the flame licked into the air, blue and red cow tongues licking the black air, cowlicks of flame, when the heat of it had become intense and almost unbearable, tears flowed down my cheeks because I was not sure I could continue to fight. It occurred to me that I might only lie down and be overtaken. It seemed somehow easier, skin rising, the heat of it comforting. Yes, it would be, eventually. It seemed a simple solution to a problem the particulars of which at that moment eluded me. At this point, I was pulled back, away from the shifting path of fire.

It was Willem, taller than I remembered him, as if suddenly he was a real person who had before been a vague figment of my imagination. Perspiration ran through his hair and down his face, and there was a swipe of black dirt over the bridge of his nose. His jeans were loose on him and barely hung around his torso, that torso that I had so recently hung around. I think I smiled at him or at least at the memory of our limbs entwined and the rush, the memory of the long rush of orgasm that pulsed at my uterus and down the conduit of my vagina. I did smile at him.

I love you, he said, then.

I'm sure I did smile at him.

He looked so sure of himself, and I wondered if that had something to do with the way I had been so overtly fighting this menace, if that had propelled him to feel something he could only describe, and aloud, as love. He had been working behind me, and through the dark and the flicker of fire, he may have caught glimpses of my bending form, the curve of my flank, the lifting, rising of my figure, which may have reminded him of us earlier in the day, which may, in turn, have reminded him of something comforting, a mothering caress of long ago, perhaps, and the urge to express that in terms all the world might understand overwhelmed him and he pulled me back and dared to say, I love you.

I can't live without you. Come with me. I will be the honest woodcutter.

I hope I smiled. Such a kind man. Maudlin, I know, but much of life is.

No, I answered. It's just a story. It isn't real.

We could make it so.

This is real, I said, pointing to the fire dancing through the duff. He pushed an orange strand of hair out of my face; his face was looming at me in a way that distorted it.

No, I said. I can't.

Why not?

It would become real, I said.

I did not know much at the time. Did not know the future,

could not read it in any signs that may or may not have been evident at that time to read. I did not know that every aspect of my little hopes and dreams would become suddenly unachievable, even the infantile desire for dreams and dreaming would leave me, and that everything I knew, all this was in the process of falling away from me. I could not even imagine then how my life could unravel. Willem called me crazy-girl again and I began to half believe him. He took my arm and put it around his waist as if I was a doll he could manipulate.

Crazy, he said, I thought you liked me.

I like you, I said.

Marry me. I could stay here then. Stay in Canada. Stay in you too. Such a beautiful country.

It was a consolation to know that aspects of his feelings for me were sullied by his dream of immigration. It held the sad notion of lost opportunity in check. There was no one whose desire did not infiltrate his values. No cloth that did not stain. I felt the warm earth edging toward my boots as we kissed that last time.

Clara had been taken back to camp with a respiratory problem. We were all soot and fire-grease and sweat. Paul was panting and giggling hysterically, the cuffs of his pants charred by the flame. It was three a.m. when the last whorl of smoke evaporated into the sky. We were waiting for Ortwin to return and fetch us. The night was hot, the still-hot soil radiated an uncanny, unsettling warmth. Willem came up behind me and ran his half finger along my arm and then up the centre of my back, my spine. Osho was sitting cross-legged beside me. I was not certain whether he was awake. Then he sighed.

It will need to be replanted, he said. He was utterly worn out.

Yes, said Paul, always look on the bright side. Osho tossed a clump of debris at him. A petulant, tired gesture, no more than that.

A subtle waft of air lifted the cinders in a swirling pattern that threatened but did not overstep the landscape of the burn, a circle of ash. Upon looking here into this motion of blackened dust and air, I felt I knew some things that I had never before considered. Willem's maimed finger up my back and the crew standing, kneeling, sitting about exhausted had a morbid weight. It was the atmosphere of nothingness, of waiting, and within it all possibility. There was a collective wonderment, all of us looking into this swirl of ash.

Ortwin eventually returned, his purple slacks luminescent in their cleanliness, in the light of the moon, and told us that the money we thought might have been earned by our noble firefighting work was not to be. He wasn't even planning to report the fire. Apparently, the company would be fined for starting the fire if this was discovered; the contract might be entirely voided because of our carelessness. In short, he had duped us. We heard the rustle but could not see a grouse searching about for whatever she had lost. We had witnessed fire. Ortwin led us out through the night to the crummies. The gear was heavier on the way out. If we had known we were working for free, would we have bothered? Or would we have simply left the fire to rise and build into a magnificent, crackling, unquenchable debacle?

I woke up late the next day, the taste of soot lining my dry mouth. Ortwin had let the fire crew sleep in, and already the late morning sun warmed up the inside of my dome to an unbearable level. The stink of burnt dust. There were strange shadows cross-hatched on the roof of my tent — the swaying branches of trees? My sleeping bag had soaked up a pool of my grungy sweat, and my legs and arms lay wild, out, my body's attempt to cool itself. We were given the day off to recuperate from last night's hell, I realized. It was Ortwin's compensation. Cheap of him, but

something, at any rate. I tugged on a filthy undershirt and a pair
of boxer shorts that had the fly sewn shut, and I opened the
zipper door to my tent. And then I saw.

Willem was gone, and there was a parting gift which made
my heart beat. The cross-hatch shadows I had noticed in my tent
were formed by a web of pink tickertape wrapped around and
around it. It was a plastic spider web, wound about, coddling,
as a spider did its prey, my semi-spherical home. The pink web
trailed off to the left of my door where it twined up his dibble
shovel, dug deep into the earth. And as my eyes followed the
path of this unspeakable and unspoken story, I saw into the field
below me, where Osho and the rest slept on, web on web of
spider traps, spun in the night by thousands upon thousands of
small but real spinning spiders, all alike. Osho, Clara and Paul
would come through this field or, for all I knew, had come
through it already and were sitting in the cookshack, marvelling
at the webs softly tickling them as they broke through.

Willem was gone, his tent, his gear too. A rectangular patch
of almost dead yellow and white grass where his pup tent sat was
the only proof of his existence for the couple of weeks it took the
contract to run its course. Ortwin pulled me aside to tell me not
to take it personally, that the ministry had started asking
questions pertaining to work permits and looking at social
insurance cards. Willem had neither — was in fact working on
the SIN of a distant cousin, who had decided to take the summer
off yet still needed the weeks to qualify for unemployment
benefits — so they had decided it was better for everyone if he
left quietly.

Where exactly did he go? The vague body memory of Willem
inside me stirred me to ask.

Went to Toronto, I think, to fly out, home. He said something about a logging contract he could finish. Said he missed
the woods anyway. I have an address for him if you want.

Missed the woods, I said. That's funny.

Yeah. That is strange.

I tried not to take it personally.

We, the fire crew, took a crummy into Kapuskasing for the afternoon to rent a cheap motel room and get showered and act civilized for a couple of days. The rest of the crew would show up later in the day or the next morning. Ortwin sprang for the room, which we would share and in which we would sleep marginally less comfortably than we would have had we stayed in our tents. Osho drove. It was a shoddy, wall-to-wall-carpeted room at Riverbend Motel on Highway 11, and we took turns in the shower. The water ran black. The filth that etched my skin ran in soot and earth down my chest and legs.

The rest of the afternoon we shot pool at the Kap Inn, drank slow beers and half watched a girl dance on a small plywood platform, gyrating in a particularly learned way to a tinny extended version of "Push Push in the Bush," watched her make the sign of the cross between sets. When we got hungry, we went next door to a restaurant where once Elizabeth II sat and crumpeted, way back before my birth. We ate nicely presented burgers adorned with torn leaves of iceberg lettuce and slices of tomato imported from far away, tasteless and slightly hard.

The restaurant was essentially a huge, carpeted hall where local marriage feasts took place. It was all of a piece — the restaurant, the Kap Inn and the bar. This was the dining hall attached to the red-carpeted hotel where, years before, Karl rented a first-class room and thrust me down onto the bed. We were in the Queen's Suite, upon the very bed where Queen Elizabeth II had lain her well-coiffed head. The bedding was slightly brittle after all those years. Karl whispered his not-sweet nothings in my ear.

I like my women a little bit masculine, he muttered. And I like my men a little bit feminine. Oh, Alma! And then, his great lank of an aging body, bones everywhere, was atop me, and I laughed in shock and horror and pushed him off. He was baffled, had obviously projected a different scenario onto this occasion — the pompous sheen of red satin, that bedspread, the rarely-used-since-1951 suite, the carpet pile worn down by regular cleanings, that unsullied room, and Karl's hopes dashed.

You're an idiot, Karl, I said, pulling my shirt into place.

Yes, I know that. But even idiots need a little affection once in a while.

That was when I told him to fuck off. He smiled, reached out to brush back a wisp of my hair that had fallen along my cheek and said, It would be my pleasure, darling.

July 23. It was a pestilence sent by God's wrath, obviously. The spiders descended for a reason. I'd seen Willem leave. Ortwin's miserable little cowboy drove him off, and I thought good riddance to bad rubbish. Cloud of golden dust, and he was gone. I geared up and sat waiting in the crummy. I had missed a fire, I heard. Slept right through a little cataclysm. More proof, of course. And I was back in the field while the rest slept in. I was racing my trees into the ground as if the very wind had befriended me. I washed carefully that night; I would see her in town the next day. Back at the Kap Inn where first we . . .

Osho, Paul, Clara and I stumbled out of the bar late, stood mesmerized in the parking lot. Across the Kapuskasing River the pulp mill was a sight to behold, Spruce Falls all lit up, spewing a thick cloud of sour, yeasty-smelling smoke from its stacks. It was the year of the hundred millionth planted tree. The mill was celebrating. The yellow and grey clouds of exhaust undulated in patterns, smoke divination. I was drunk, the lights were blurred by my skewed vision, my swaying body. I was in awe of this beauty. Clara coughed. The smoke of the previous day had affected her lungs, and in coughing, she broke my reverie.

Lovely industry, said Paul. Really marvellous.

What?

Osho brought us back to the motel, concentrating hard to keep the crummy in a straight line. And I fell asleep, the memory of fire licking air lulled me, in a bed with Clara, although when I woke up she was nestled with Paul on the other bed. Osho slept in the bathtub. They said I was thrashing but I remembered nothing, only the green baize of the pool table and the clack of ball on ball — a repeating dream of no importance.

Chapter Eighteen

Jake comes back in the night. I do not hear him latch the door nor wrap a rope around this latch to lock us in. Safely. I do hear his lusty snores, which wake me; rectilinear shafts of light enter, prettily framing his filthy, age-shrunk head. Dust motes burst from his mouth with each exhalation; if I look closely can I read them? I wonder where he has been. He wakes up when I prod him with the handle of an old broom he's made with an alder branch. Half in his sleep, he announces that we've got to work in the garden.

Everything sorts itself out if you take care of nature, he says.

He compliments my soup too. He's talkative. I'm sure he's covering something up. Talking — the great firewall. I'll let him talk and talk. The bugs have eased off, and we are pulling back aisles of carpeting in order to clean them and then replant the corridors with late crops of spinach, radish, more lettuce. The carpeting harbours colonies of woodlice, which fall off and scatter, at once camouflaged by the dirt. The ground is packed down where we have trodden, but poking through are worms and worm-like roots. While we work, we are disturbing households.

For weeks and months, I walked around as if I was dead, he says. My sea legs stayed with me. My balance was shifting. The solid earth was all liquid and I could not get the picture of her sprawled body out of my head. I didn't feel responsible. I tried to but I couldn't. I'll admit to being changed. Before I was determined. After I was nothing. I wandered around for years, working here and there and everywhere, doing whatever people wanted me to do. Hand to mouth, hand to mouth. This was the way I saw the world. I found one day I was up here. I did some jobs in the mines but never anything too ambitious. I liked it in the earth, this was not the problem. The problem was I was unreliable. The problem was I did not like to live up to expectations. I did not like to be expected and so, often, I did not come to work. And sometimes too the walls of the mines worried me. I was not afraid but I felt dead. Buried. And so I wandered away for a time until I felt better. You brought your sadness here, he says. He's agitated.

I say, No, Jake. No, not at all. Now I wish he would shut up.

I walked deep in the forest yesterday, he says. I walked deeper than ever until I did not know the trees around me. I could feel the animals moving away from me because they were cautious. I was thinking if there might be a smell of man, something of our work, a stink of business that warns them away. I could hear them everywhere. In the parks in the city, the chipmunks, the squirrels and the little birds will become bold. I have seen them come to eat cookies out of the hands of people. You sit down, very still, and you hold your hand out and they come eventually to eat. But this is a trick, isn't it? This is bringing the animal into the world of men, not the other way around. It is no better than keeping a bird in a cage and teaching it to speak English. We conquer, men do. They smell it, the stink of it sweating out of our bodies. And they run away for the little pockets of wilderness they can at least pretend are still theirs.

I . . .

No.

But . . .

No. Shh. I walked deeper still into the forest, and while I walked I was deep in thought and not really paying attention to where I was. The woods were very thick and I was having some trouble moving through the pines, the dead branches whipped

me as I passed. The light was less and less and then it was wet
darkness. I shivered and looked around me. I am old, I thought
all of a sudden, though I don't usually think about that ever. I
am, that's all. Stands of three and four trees grew together. It was
good. There was only a spongy floor of red and brown needles
and the good smell of decay and the trees, here and there; they
are in conversation, I think, and this thought makes me smile.
Then I got a bit scared. I was really deep in.

Jake . . .

Listen, he says, staring me down. I was in the true wilderness
where no man has yet corrupted. I stood and smiled and I was
so cold with my good humour, and then by chance I glanced
down again and something shone up at me. It was a rock full of
mica, maybe. And I crouched. But it wasn't a rock. It was the end
of a little silver spoon, marked with the maker's seal. It's sterling
and decorated with a leaf pattern. I was not afraid anymore, and
I laughed a bit until the smile froze on my face. I thought about
her again then. You wanted me to think about her, and I need
you to know that you have your heart's desire; now I began to
think back in time to her. The fat lady from the *Titanic* is there
before me like a sick ghost. There in the deepest woods, de-
manding answers. She was swaying, leaning against the swaying
of her berth, the stand of trees. I thought suddenly, was her name
perhaps Bertha? A joke to divert my attention from her anger.
I saw right then, in the forest, that you were right. I saw with
the flash of this silver spoon in the heart of the woods that I had
abandoned her, that I'd miscalculated my inconsequence. I had
not acted, only reacted.

Yes?

I failed at living.

That's a bit much.

No. Come, he says, and picks up Adam. Come. He takes us
to the mine pit and points at the gravel beach. There is a note
scratched out there. I cannot make out any of the words, only

single letters, f, z, qu, and when I ask Jake about it, he shrugs and says he can't see them at all.

How do you know, then?

He told me.

Who told you?

I take to circumnavigating the pit every day, widdershins. There have been no ramifications. The time for me to leave this place will soon end and I will have forced a decision to stay another year. I have grown fond of Jake, though that is not what binds me. I am uncertain what I should do if I return home. I will no sooner arrive than all sorts of requirements will be made of me. I will be asked to engage in conversation for the sake of same. This thought in itself is wearying. My mother will wish to know all the details of my motherhood. I will have to lie or half-lie, which is, in its intimacy, worse. I wish the letters spelled out some runic answer to these questions which eat at me. I glance out into the impenetrable forest and shout obscenities that diminish infinitely into the treed space. Fuck off, I yell. And, What? Why? And especially, over and over, I yell, What did I do to deserve this?

The weaving is almost done. My work is near finished. If not for Jake and my mother I would leave as soon as this task is completed.

Burchard's wound, sewn together, had healed into a thin white scar. When Renelde saw him, which was seldom, he reminded her of Guilbert. And that he was gone. She would have neither a dishonest man nor an honest man, and so she settled into a life alone, the same life she supposed her mother to have led, small comfort. Occasionally

she went gleaning into the forest, her grandmother
now too old and tired to do much but sup and sit
and sleep, like a cat, in and out of dream throughout the day and night. The great-grandmother was a
benign cipher in the corner, eating next to nothing,
seldom speaking except to transmit some old wives'
tale or ancient irrelevant fairy story.

Renelde gathered young shoots and nuts to be
cooked up or preserved for healing salves, teas and
pottage. For the purpose of gathering, she had a
basket that she had made from bent willow shoots.
As she wandered through the forest, Renelde felt,
on occasion, watched. She put this down to phantom memories and wild creatures hiding. If she
saw Burchard, she would swiftly shift herself into
whatever foliage provided itself and she would hide
— but the hiding was other, having something to
do with watching as well as something to do with
not being seen. She was not a fawn escaping cap-
ture. She was interested in Burchard, curious about
him — his anger, his wealth, his presence, his help-
lessness to resist her weaving. It was important that
he not see her there, mortally important. She held
the basket low, out of the way.

Renelde saw how old he had become through
his long illness. His nastiness was betrayed by his
sallow skin, the barely flickering life in his eyes.
He acted at times as if he knew he was not alone,
checking over his shoulder and chortling. He wore
shining breeches, black. What cloth were they?

You wench! he cried, looking about him. He
might have lost his mind. The fever *had* been long
and arduous, and he had certainly come to be an

old man. I see you, he yelled, his chin thrust out in defiance, petulance. Why do you torment me so? Coquette!

The spoon that Jake brought back from the forest was caked in earth but, when washed in sand, came out more beautiful than anyone could have hoped. We strung it from the overhang, a sort of lonely chime outside the door. It has disappeared. This is a pity because the shiny cutlery gave Adam untold pleasure. He pointed at it. Day after day he reached out to grab at it and, finding that it moved, laughed and laughed. It is gone. I have told Jake that the boy found it too distracting and that I've put it away. Jake says I am pleasureless in the face of my own child's pleasure. He accuses me of jealousy. I am jealous. Jealous of the way his fat arms, fat on my milk, by the way, reach out in joy toward that object. But I am jealous even more when the spoon goes missing. For someone *has* taken it. No bear pulls up on hind legs for crow's booty. The string was untied as carefully as can be; the slender twine is sullied. It hangs empty, a fairy noose. I am undone.

Adam, when I carry him across the threshold, wails for the missing spoon, as if he is in mortal pain, and now, instead of up, he reaches out, toward the black forest, toward the culprit. I think to leave him bundled at the forest edge and be done. I *am* undone. When Jake runs away again, I vow I will do it. I will wander over close to that place. I can feel myself melt into the vision of another as I draw near. I disappear into those eyes. But Jake is stubborn. He stays and stays.

You never go, I say.

Garden.

Supplies? I try.

That's okay. We'll manage.

One day, I hear the thrum of a faraway bird, and it comes nearer. I realize it is a machine, not a bird. The Doppler effect runs through me as if the quad itself knocked me down and killed me. I stand stock-still as it hurtles past the clearing. It is a man and a woman, the wind pulls their long hair out behind them. I see she is clutching him more tightly than she needs to. She is wearing a yellow T-shirt and they are in love. If I run and holler and wave, they will hear me and return to rescue me and Adam. We do not need rescuing. There is no hidden spot, no bad, no good, no need to rescue nothing from nothing. I feel the forest suck in its breath and pretend it is not there. They pass by again minutes later, and I am inexplicably remorseful.

Let's stop, I hear her say.

But the young man doesn't hear, or does not want to hear.

I turn to the shack and see Jake's frightened face peering out the window. I wonder if he looked so curiously worried when it was Willem and me, not passing but stopping, invading his concealment.

What was that? he says.

That was history repeating itself, I say. But he doesn't laugh.

July 25. They stole my book so I'm forced to scribble in the sand. At night. I almost had a heart attack today when a vehicle tore through the place. I was just eating, you see, I'd stolen a bit of mash from the shack when they were in the garden, the window was open. I was settled back in the bush huddled over my bowl with the beautiful spoon. I love the silver spoon. It's lovely to eat in a civilized fashion after all this time. The spoon lends a dignity to all this mucking about in the woods. An obnoxious couple flew by on a quad and I choked and almost, well, I felt my heart constrict in a horrific way, as if it might go out. Imagine if the heart truly broke. I suddenly imagined it. The little boy has touched this spoon, you know. I can't wait to touch him. Soon. Courage. Courage.

Chapter Nineteen

I did not pine for Willem after he left. He stayed with me, a phantom limb by my side, while I planted my last thousand thousand trees, the bags filling, this unbearable weight gradually lightening until I felt almost buoyant. In losing him, I had also lost the babysitting per diem that came with him. This forced me to plant faster. I had two weeks for my last hurrah — I wanted to get out of this with ten grand, that was my goal. Karl contrived to plant near me, and every once in a while he yelled encouragement.

Jezebel!

No matter how fast I planted, I could not compete. I sensed him breathing down my neck. He planted as if he was pursuing me, chasing me up and down the corridors in a way that would have appeared, bird's eye, as a strange game with a multiplicity of rules. Karl was it. He leered at me through the wild rose and fireweed and the grass that was by now the height of harvestable wheat.

I see you.

I'm working, Karl. I'm trying to work, okay?

He pulled alongside me and slowed his pace so that for ages I couldn't lose him. Increasing my speed proved impossible (I was incapable of going any faster), so I tried slowing down until I might as well stop, might as well unplant. He planted and stood up and stared at me. The salt sweat and caustic garlic reek of him wafted over. He rubbed his eyes with the balls of his loose fists in a kind of Tourette's tic as if he never quite believed what he saw. His eyes were rheumy from constant rubbing.

You're lovesick, he said. I can tell.

I don't think so, Karl.

No use denying. It's written all over your body language. I thought you were a little smarter than that, eh? Eh? I mean this idea of the noble savage, this wild boy of Aveyron, this whatever you call it, Iron Hans, Jungle Boy silliness is all pretty old fashioned, out of date. Like a hundred years or so out of date. I mean you didn't really seriously think about it like that, did you?

What are you talking about?

I was there, he said. I saw you and Ideal Man, eh? Thumping about in the forest like two little lovebirds. I almost began clapping my hands. Yes? It was very Romantic with a capital R. I must think about the Grimm brothers going around collecting all that crap, that folklore, the fairy stories, eh? And good old Friedrich Froebel walking around with his kindergartners in the Black Forest. I too love the noble savage. He is so-o-o nostalgic. But really we must draw the line when it comes to selection. I had such high hopes for us, Alma, you have no idea.

Go away, will you?

The Hapsburg dynasty, he continued. Well, I realize that there isn't a wooden nickel left, but there is something in a name, a pedigree at the very least, don't you agree? I know eugenics is not really politically correct. However, I could have given you such well-bred children, Alma. Instead you insist on seeking out the primitive. I get such a headache, you know? Karl rubbed his fingers together, his bulbous fingers that looked like those of a tree frog, and pressed the balls of his hands into his eye sockets, alleviating some pressure within. The pressure of his own personality.

I don't understand, I said. Some instinct buried deep within me suggested I should run but I held it at bay, willing to examine it only as if it were not really part of me, an alien thought of no consequence. Make him stop. But no.

I had you there years ago in the Queen's Suite, Alma. I'm insensitive, I'll admit to that. I thought I had reason to entertain the idea that you might reciprocate. I am an idiot in that case — you were right there. I don't expect you to easily forget and forgive this, no. But if I had been my own ancestor, ho ho, I would have just proceeded. How times have changed! I would have simply raped you. There were plenty of fine, well-adjusted children born in those good old days under just these circumstances. So you can admit that I'm maybe slightly better than my legacy. I mean I didn't do it, you agree, and now I want to apologize for that.

Forget it, Karl. Just . . .

I'm not really finished, he said. Karl's voice had become a bit wheezy, and certain bits of what he had to say went missing in the gaps that memory defined. He grabbed my shoulder with his free hand, so strong for such a weak man, I thought, and I could already feel the surge of adrenaline through my limbs, but I did not run. I was paralyzed by what might be his intentions. I could see the whites of his eyes all around the irises.

What about Kaspar Hauser?

Karl . . .

All Kaspar could say the whole time was, "I want to be a rider like my father," over and over again. What about the wild boy of Aveyron, or better, Wild Peter, found in seventeen-something-or-other in Hanover with nothing at all to say? Completely retarded, I suppose, sucking the iron and minerals out of a stalk of nettle, eh? You don't think you can escape this, do you? You don't think I can see through you, either. I can see right into your heart. It's deluded. Karl was shaking me lightly, and I thought I might faint but didn't. He wouldn't shut up.

He muttered under his stinking breath, Look at you. And you will keep on until there isn't anything left for you at all. The world is not as pretty as you imagine, Alma. It isn't a story or something with a nice ending. There is no remedy for what ails us. This is only yearning. Poof — it's gone! And now I am going to save you from this delusion so that you will maybe make something of yourself.

Stop it, Karl. Let me go.

But I love you already for a long time.

You're crazy.

There is nothing more pure than action, he announced. You will accept this in time. And don't forget. If you do, I will be back to remind you. He let me go then, and after glaring at me for a moment, he stepped over the slash and got back to work. He didn't talk to me for the rest of the day, but there was an uneasiness in the air.

July 28. I almost ruined everything that day. I almost did but not quite. I couldn't help my melodrama, you must try to understand, I was born out of time. I scared her. She had no idea what I was on about and thought I was crazy. I'm not, of course. You know that. I have you as my witness, then. I repented over and over again to her. I think she had forgiven me. I think she accepted my apology. I was so sorry. Very, very, very. My intensity can be scary.

Chapter Twenty

I cannot abandon Adam. Jake watches every move I make and besides has taken to carting the boy with him when he is out of my sight. When I protest he says I am unfit. Says I don't take precautions against hungry predators. I am housebound. I am good for nothing except weaving and sewing. I see that Jake has sharpened his knife. We have not eaten meat in weeks. I've noticed Jake holding the walls for guidance and patting the ground in the garden to locate plants.

Is this a weed, Alma?

Yes, Jake. Plantain.

For bruising.

Yes.

He wraps his fingers around the stalk and wiggles it until it is loose enough to yank. Instead of hunting, he has taken to sharpening his weapon. It is part of the inertia of his identity and suffices. I'm hungry, but out of kindness, I do not mention the lack of meat.

The latest panel is bordered with diamonds and features a woodlouse and a lively little fly. I have begun to sew the pieces together and I'm pleased with the result.

    ⚘ Two years passed and Burchard was sick again. No one lives forever, though some seek to. He was ill. His natural time had come. His body became wasted, a skeleton housed in gossamer skin. The illness had progressed until Burchard lay upon his

deathbed, but still the end would not approach.
It awaited him like a shy maiden, tormented him.
He could not move without searing pains shooting
through every piece of him.

Agony. He coughed up blood mixed with some
black horror he had no energy to hide; he spat it
on the floor by his bed, where it lay for one of his
servants to clean up. Unceasingly, the countess
prayed for him. But Burchard beckoned death,
calling out in the night for an end to his earthly
bonds. Death maintained her own schedule, and
he lived on.

Let me die! Take me.

Renelde's loom sat idle in the hut. The shroud
cloth, which was that close to completion, sat
under two years of accumulated dust, dust mixed
with the remains of moths and other insects —
mosquitoes, midges, June bugs — which had been
drawn into the hut by day, or by the occasional
flicker of a candle by night. These small creatures
perished above the halted work in such a way that
the intricate weaving was hidden; the entire story
that Renelde had so cunningly portrayed, picture
by picture, was buried beneath them. No one went
into that corner of the hut anymore. It was as if a
taboo emanated from it; it was a sepulchre.

The idea of it, of the nearly finished winding
sheet, rose up like a ghost and grew meaningful
in the mind of the dying man — how could he
be dying but never dead? An esoteric connection
came to him, and he signalled to the servant standing closest to him, grabbed the man's leg, in fact,
and almost toppled him over.

Tell the girl to finish the shroud, he muttered.

Do this now. He collapsed onto his bed and would have slept if the cough had not caught him first. The room stank.

To convince Renelde to begin, it took a visit from the countess — she who abhorred the notion that Renelde could possibly control the hand of death. It was superstitious, a deception, a sinful thought. But she couldn't stand to see her man suffer, couldn't stand any sort of suffering. In truth it made her sick to her stomach.

Will he consent to the marriage? That was what the girl dared to ask. How quickly worldliness gave wisdom. The countess missed the perplexed expression on Renelde's face, saw only her duplicity.

For me, Renelde, for God's sake, I plead. For the sake of your poor mother's grave. And Renelde had to acquiesce. She would do anything for the countess, well, anything but alter the story. And since she was not asked to do this, she sighed and consented. She did not dust the cloth for fear the stratum of dead bugs and dust mites would penetrate and damage the material, and, of course, she could not disengage the shroud from the loom until completion, could not shake it out at all. So she worked carefully so as not to disturb the small corpses lying there, the new cloth reflecting the little light cast by the hearth fire, growing next to the old, its surface dull and invisible beneath the debris.

The cloth was wet with her tears as she worked the final little stories into it. The entire process took but a week, and as she cut the cloth from the loom, sewed up the ends, she felt an urgency to her work. The two guards, who had not so very long before tied her to rocks and sought to drown her, escorted her to Burchard's bedside to present the strange sheet and receive a final kiss and watch life slip away. The bells began immediately to toll for the man's demise. The last woven tableau was hidden as she stood there, clutched in the smooth adolescent skin of her fingers. It was a full self-portrait, one of her hands holding the cloth of her dress up, the look in her eyes an ambiguous mixture of fear and love, the other hand over her belly. This tableau represented a recent event, one that had transpired a week before Burchard the Wolf had taken ill the second time.

She had moved so casually in the thicket beneath his horse that he might not have seen her and would not have had the sighting not been intentional. She gasped when their eyes met, suddenly unsure why she had let herself be seen. He slid from the stallion.

Well, what have we here?

He kissed her; she let him. She ran her fingers down the lappet of his brocaded vest and around the silk-covered buttons and further down, unexpectedly down the cool of his breeches, the silk enticing her. Under the canopy of the hundred-year-old beeches and oaks, the cloth of his richesse, slippery and luxurious against her skin. She found the laces on his breeches easily undone. She pulled the cloth of his shirt, tearing it along the warp, destroying it simply because she wanted to hear the sound of cloth ripping. Creatures unable to find their age-old paths climbed over their legs but they did not feel this. The bower of the forest provided her with this one secret.

Upon his death, his last words were, Let Renelde marry her stupid woodcutter.

Renelde's story decayed quickly beneath the earth, nettle cloth being far more unstable than the seemingly more fragile silk. Small animals bored minuscule holes through it to get at the cadaver, but in so doing they slowly obliterated the story until only remnants of it were left, and these disintegrated too until not one thread could ever be unearthed. Of course Guilbert came back. He was there before the funeral-day vespers, claiming what was his. As soon as the bells began to toll for the death of Burchard the Wolf, Guilbert emerged and took his place beside Renelde, well back from the throng of revellers who hid their joy in solemn faces and sidelong winks. Her stomach jumped at the sight of him yet she wasn't unhappy. The stench of two years in the bush gave him a beastly reek, but his presence assured the future legitimacy of the other worry that lurched within her.

Chapter Twenty-One

The last day of the contract ran late. The block had to be fully planted out and so Ortwin instructed us to push the spacing to eight feet. The last few trays seemed to multiply even as we claimed them, and it was after seven before I popped my last container-stock pot into the ground. I tied a ribbon to that tree and did a little dance around it, whooping and caterwauling with the others. My feet were light as I walked my gear out to the road. We drank beer and wound Paul and Clara up in ticker-tape. Joe and Ed were goosing each other and squealing. I felt my shoulders soften as the aches from weeks of labour descended upon me. It was as if my joints no longer had cartilage between them. Karl stood off to the side with a strange unflinching smile on his face.

Cheers, he said, raising his beer bottle toward mine.

Bug off.

He said, To morality, then. A toast! Everyone!

Nobody bothered with him. Was he there? His foul odour, his crass presentation, his numerous sexual advances, his impropriety. I walked over, smiling, and pushed him with both my hands, and he lost whatever precarious balance he had on the surface of the earth and fell over into the sand-dusted weeds at the side of the road.

Paul said, Perfect, Alma, now he'll really think you like him.

Raise a toast. Joe and Ed hoisted their beer in the air.

To Garlic Karlic!

Whoohoo . . .

Karl's eyes bulged slightly and then he started to laugh, a laugh of hearty joy. He had managed not to spill a drop of beer in the fall. The vans started up and we piled in and still he laughed, although his laughter was drowned out by puttering motors, the squeak of drive shafts engaging. He scrambled in at the last minute, brushing dust off his jeans, moving to the back, pitching comically to and fro with the jerky motion of the van.

The party went on into the night, ending sometime in the wee hours with Joe and Ed and Paul doing a striptease on one of the fold-out cafeteria tables. Osho sat morosely in the corner, trying to pretend he wasn't bothered that Marilene was laughing and dancing to the music that whined out of the tinny ghetto blaster, naked men around her. I drank too much and let Karl walk with me to my tent. He held me steady and put his hand out once to lift me when I fell. I found everything strangely funny — his large hand, the gesture of help, his awkward face, the waft of garlic, that I should even let him walk with me — and I laughed until the tears ran down my face. He cried, I recall, he joined in my mirth and laughed until he cried. And he unzipped my tent and helped me in and zipped the arch up again, and I heard his dying footsteps as he retreated to the cookshack and the party, a perfect gentleman. I pulled my clothes off and was asleep as my head touched the air mattress. I slept for a time, and when I awoke I could no longer hear the sounds of festivity.

The night was still and I lay there wondering what had awakened me. There were already light particles in the air. Morning was near. First I thought that perhaps the light woke me, but then I heard it: scratching and a rustling of plastic. It must be an early morning squirrel and I tapped at the inside of my tent. It was no squirrel. The thing bounded off heavily into the forest. Another moose? I pulled on a T-shirt and tugged the zipper open. I looked about for tracks, and when I could not find any I began to walk into the brush in the hope of seeing the beast. I kept my head down looking for tracks, wanting to discover the direction in which the animal had fled. It was not until he grabbed at my arm that I realized.

He swung his other arm around me and covered my mouth just in time to muffle my scream. He was so drunk the pong of booze masked the garlic.

I see you have forgotten, he said.

Let me go.

Think about Rumpelstiltskin, he said. He was clutching at me, trying to push me to the ground even as I struggled against him.

Just calm down, Karl, and go to your own tent, okay?

I didn't scream.

You know the story I'm sure, he muttered. It's not new to you. Stupid peasant tells the king his daughter can spin straw into gold; stupid king believes this in spite of himself. He locks her in a room and tells her to spin up his straw. Who cares if the peasant girl is neither beautiful nor well born? He's going to be the richest man in the world. Well, that girl cries and cries until this ugly little dwarf comes to save her. Then ol' Rumpel does all this work for her, spinning straw into gold thread, and all for the sake of a child, something to call his own. But man cannot have a child by himself, not even a really randy bastard like me. Rumpel is nothing without a girl, and who would have him? He's disgusting. You agree with me here. He smells like rotting compost. And he's a shit disturber too. But the history books are full of women outsmarting men. Rumpelstiltskin is nothing new, history repeats itself, et cetera et cetera et cetera. It's no wonder we men are so brutal. Without you, we'd have no hope of evolving.

Karl? You don't want to do this. I mumble through his fingers. The taste of earth and garlic pressed into my mouth. I could not pull my arm away. The clutch became more convincing as his fingers pressed into me. There were tears in his eyes, and eventually these tears began to stream down his face. I struggled to get away from him, but his arms were stronger than mine. He held me with a power I couldn't imagine someone possessing, pushed me onto the forest floor, into the scat of thousands of years of little forest creatures. In my half-drunken lucid state, I wondered if this was a bad dream from which I would never awake. I kicked at him but his strength was brutal. He held me down with the length of his body, his hand again over my mouth, his bulbous finger pushed in between my lips, and he pulled his trousers off halfway down his legs, pushed my legs apart. He dryly bumped against my cervix. I tried to turn away and shut my mind to what he was doing. I left myself. I played dead. Something along the ground rubbed against the scab that had finally grown over the nettle wound on my shoulder and scratched it open until it bled. And all the while I could hear him breathing, could smell the rankness of him, so that the words he spoke, the drink and the garlic became one association.

I'm sorry.

I'm sorry.

I'm sorry, he said. All I ever wanted was something to call my own, you know. It isn't asking for too much. I just can't help it.

July 29. Can't you see, I loved her? I loved her indecision, I loved her resistance, I loved where the bugs had bitten her, where the treebags had formed a callus around her waist, the muff of hair like a small creature, the everything of her everything. Can't you see?

Chapter Twenty-Two

It started raining yesterday. Jake and I are holed up inside and I am telling him "The Nettle Spinner." I glance outside and all I see is a wall of rain. I've finished up the weaving and almost run out of thread. In fact, the last panel I fudged. It is foreshortened for lack of nettle, the figures distorted. Still they are strangely compelling. Renelde is horrid, no proper torso and badly rendered, tiny, ridiculous legs. I'm quickly sewing the panels together when we hear a banging at the door. Well, it starts out as a banging and then degenerates into a scratching, as if someone or something is writing along the rude wooden surface. This cannot be, and were we brave people we would get up and investigate. As it is, Jake pulls the blanket up over himself and Adam and begins to moan.

I knew it. I knew it, he cries.

I drop down and crawl over to him, whispering instructions.

I will stay with the baby. He is skeptical at first but I keep telling him over and over until he begins to nod automatically. I am grinning at his compliance. I see he is grinning too. All will be well.

The bear has arrived, I say.

Ah!

The bear. The bear.

It may be a wolf?

Imagine it is a bear and this will give you strength.

It *is* a man, he says. He whimpers and holds the baby as if he's a talisman.

No, no, no. An oversized black bear hunting the baby. It is in the habit of stealing our food. It has found our dump. Jake. Listen to me. You have to act. You have to act right now. You have to kill it. You have to. Jake, please. For the sake of . . .

There is silence for a time and the rain washes our fears away only slowly. After some minutes it seems as if nothing happened, and we begin to let down our guard. Only I haven't. I know it is false comfort. The bear will return for Adam, I whisper. High drama; work on his sentiment. And I am right. The scratching starts again. I rub my hand up and down Jake's arm. He is terrified!

I can't see, he whines. He tries this. But he knows that I know he can find his way, blind or not. He certainly sees my point.

I say, The little spoon, Jake! The little spoon has gone missing.

I see he is crying, that I've hit a soft spot. Jake is mine now. I know it.

And from then on, it is over quickly. Come, I whisper. He rolls the baby in the blanket and follows me to my bedroom, watches as I pull the screen out of the window. A faint, sliding noise of wood on wood, nothing more. I give Jake a leg up to the window, and he is so quiet even I am impressed. Death comes to all things, does it not? I hear him moving around the shack, and I move slowly inside the shack tracing his small sounds; if I did not know he was there, I would have heard nothing. There is a barely audible thumping, the slick sharp blade of Jake's knife, well placed. Beyond the regular shushing of rain against the roof, the ground, the tink against the window, I hear the sound of dragging, the sound of dead resistance, of form against earth, as if it already seeks to claim its due. Jake returns, banging at the door to get in, and when I open it he goes back to his heap of skins, his bed, and huddles under the blanket with Adam, shivering and keening.

Where did you put it?

It is beneath the bedroom window here. It was a man.

No, Jake. You're wrong about that. I can smell bear. It's a bear.

Or a wolf? he says.

Timber wolves are very big.

Do they come around here?

Yes. Haven't we seen them?

By morning the flies have gathered; I have put the screen back in and they are creeping up it inside my bedroom, clustering inside the shack. Born of nothing, old wood, they have arrived here with ominous spontaneity. They press and press and crawl upon one another in a vain attempt to escape this house. Their liveliness is astounding, reminding me of my own.

I rouse Jake after I've nursed the boy back to sleep. The flies have multiplied and it has become difficult to see out the window. Jake's eyes flutter and close again.

No.

Yes. The flies . . .

No.

I can't do it alone, I say. The nettle sheet is tucked under my shirt; my plan is unfolding perfectly.

Let it rot there, he says.

It will stink. You have to help me finish this. The crows will come, the creatures will come. We can't have that, you know. They'll eat the garden next. I keep prodding him until he gets out of the bed. He is moaning and keening under his breath. His eyes are tearing, and I think how strange it is to see this stream of feeling dripping from opaque eyes. I pull him outside and around to the body. We each grab an ankle and tug the thing as far into the bush as seems necessary. I send him back for the shovel, and as he digs I take the cloth, the nettle cloth, and slide the outer edges under the body. It is simple to flip him over and over until he is entirely wrapped. By the end of it, the material is filthy with his dirt and the muddied earth upon which he lies. He has not begun to rot at all. Jake is sobbing. The shovel tings against the rock shield of my country, which protects itself from this sort of sullying by its very impenetrability. He hasn't got more than two feet down but that will have to do. It is a lazy, careless burial.

What did you say?

Nothing.

By the end of the day, we hear the screaming of ravens. I think I see one flying up, up, a fragment of cloth flapping from its beak. Soon there will be nothing. I don't hear Jake after a while and I look around. He's gone from here, disappeared into the woods maybe. His deep resonant moaning has stopped. Beside me, the baby reaches up toward the dust hanging in the air and gurgles, oblivious. He begins to cry, quickly gathering his anxiety into something beyond my small capacity to soothe. I try bouncing him in my arms but it doesn't help. I coo. I nurse. He is disconsolate, inconsolable. Colic? I find I am crying in the face of my uselessness. I will pack him up; I will head out toward civilization. The great anticlimax. My crying is cold and tearless.

Waa, waa. The boy won't stop.

Waa, waa. It hits every nerve ending.

I say. I say. I say, I yell, I'm faultless. I never did anything. Adam stops and stares and resumes. And then I recall the book. It is tucked under a board in the kitchen. I build a little fire outside. It sputters and threatens to go out, but while it smokes and coughs for life, I go in and fetch the little journal, for that is what it is. I toss it in the fire, which rises in a brief expression of flame and then dies again.

I look in the boy's mouth while he wails and see a sharp white stone. He has cut his first tooth.

Acknowledgements

It was a fascination with the fairy tale "The Nettle Spinner" (Andrew Lang's *The Red Fairy Book*) that led me to this retelling. I am indebted to the late Margaret Hald for her article "The Nettle as a Culture Plant" and to Elizabeth Wayland Barber for her book *Women's Work: The First 20,000 Years: Women, Cloth and Society*. I wish to acknowledge the late Joan Bodger for simply being Joan Bodger.

Thank you to my agent, Hilary McMahon, and Westwood Creative Artist; and to Goose Lane Editions, especially Laurel Boone and Susanne Alexander. I am grateful to Dawne McFarlane, Christine Fischer Guy, Brian Panhuyzen and Lewis DeSoto for thoughtful readings of early drafts of this novel. I would like to thank Lynne Douglas, for sharing her expertise on portable looms, and Rosemary Wallbank, Cheryl Wiebe and Ida Marie Threadkell, the nettle spinners of Salt Spring Island, British Columbia; any errors herein should be attributed to fanciful rendering on my part. Thank you to Tim Brow for graciously bantering with me on the topic of treeplanting.

I would like to thank George Murray and Ailsa Craig for their unwavering support and friendship. I am, of course, ever thankful for the steadfastness of my husband, Marc Kuitenbrouwer, and for the joy I experience through our children Linden, Jonas and Christopher.